# Julia's World Goes West

*Another Julia Deane*
*Murder Mystery*

DEBORAH M JONES

Rosehip Books

2017

*Deborah M Jones*

**The first Julia Deane murder mystery:**

**The World According to Julia (2015)**

# JULIA'S WORLD GOES WEST

DEBORAH M JONES is a retired theologian
with a doctorate in the ethical treatment of
animals. She has worked as editor for a
national newspaper and a couple of journals,
and been a teacher, lecturer, and music critic.
She is still involved in animal and
other charities and has written and
contributed to books of theology.
Apart from some drama for stage and radio,
this is her second venture into fiction.
She is passionate about
music and eighteenth-century literature, and
lives a full life in Gloucestershire.

## Rosehip Books

## 2017

*Deborah M Jones*

**Published in the UK by Rosehip Books –
www.rosehipbooks.com**

**A portion of all proceeds from the sale of this book shall go
to charity**

First Published in Great Britain in 2017 by Rosehip Books.

ISBN 13:978-1533574909

ISBN 10:1533574901

Rosehip Books, UK

**www.rosehipbooks.com**

# Chapter 1

WHAT'S THAT?

A scream?

Don't be daft.

Here, in this peaceful village?

A high-pitched sustained wail of shock.

A scream, definitely.

It was followed at once by a cacophony of barking by several dogs. Then by a loud brrrm-brrrm of a motocycle and a noisy scattering of shingle.

I dropped the bursting shopping bags back into the boot of the car, turned and ran towards the source of the sound. As I pounded down the lengthy drive towards the road, I heard the motorcycle pulling away fast from the next door drive, and speeding off on the road to my left. I sprinted to the entrance of the drive, turned right and right again and panted up the neighbours' long approach to their property. I know, a fit thirty-five-year old should not be panting from a run of a couple of hundred yards; I need more exercise, but lack the time. I know, I know....

As the drive curved, giving a view of the house, I saw the body of a man slumped over the doorstep, with two women bending over him. One called out 'Oh God' and the other shrieked loud exclamations, the sense of which I could not catch.

I yelled to them, 'Go and telephone 999. Now!'

The two looked up at me startled. The older one then disappeared into the house, towards the sound of the raucous barking, presumably to make the necessary call. The younger just stood there sobbing loudly.

As I drew near, I slowed down, dreading what I might see. With a deep breath, I bent over the body, looking for signs of life, but the man seemed utterly still. Dark red matter was oozing and dripping over and down the step onto the gravel, forming a small pool.

I straightened up and looked at the younger woman. This tall, slim, dark-haired girl just stood there, shaking and sobbing, hands covering her face. Not knowing what else to do, I stepped slowly and gingerly around the body on the threshold, and drew the girl away from the doorway deeper into the hall. I put my arms round her and hugged her close, letting her cry on my shoulder tears of shock and horror.

The older woman returned.

'The police and ambulance are on their way.'

She paused to look at the body without going closer, and I noticed she made an involuntary deep shudder. I disengaged from the young weeper, and stepped towards the older woman.

'I am Catherine Fletcher,' she said, recovering her self-composure and holding out her hand, which I shook. She turned, gesturing us to follow her to the kitchen. When we got there, she went straight through the spacious room and into an adjoining one to hush the noise of the barking dogs. They fell silent at once. She returned immediately, apologising for leaving me.

'That is my husband, Ian, lying there,' she stated, subdued and wistful. She repeated, abstractly, 'Police and ambulance are on their way.'

She paused to take a deep breath, clutching the top of a wooden kitchen chair, 'God, how awful all this is'.

She then looked up at me, 'He is dead, isn't he?'

'I rather think so,' I said, and then turned and walked back to the doorway to check, without much hope, if there were any signs of life in the stricken figure.

Shivering slightly and holding my breath, I crouched over him. Remembering the rudimentary first aid course all college teaching staff were advised to take, I placed two nervous fingertips on the part of his neck where I might feel a pulse. There was none. His stillness was absolute. I peered at the face and suddenly gagged, nausea throbbing in my throat as I noticed one open sightless eye seemingly staring at some horror beyond me. My adrenalin kicked in, a sharp frisson of fear tingling down my spine. I stood up and scanned the drive.

Was the murderous motorcyclist returning?

Birdsong was the only sound. Nature continued as if whatever happened in the world of humans was irrelevant. It was a bright day in early spring, with leaves budding and blossoms adorning several of the trees and shrubs around. A perfect day to see my first dead body, ever. I had seen photographs of corpses, but had until then been spared the sight of real live dead one – oxymoron.

Stop it. I'm not teaching now.

When my mind calmed and I stopped shaking, I took my mobile out of the shoulder bag, the long strap of which I had thrown diagonally over me, and speed-dialed my husband. After all, this was his province. Detective Inspector David Deane, one of the Met's finest murder squad officers.

He answered almost at once.

'What is it? I really can't take this call. I'm in the middle of something.'

Helpful, as ever.

'Yes, well – your parents' neighbour has just been shot. He's dead and I'm standing over the body. Surely you can take this!'

'Julia – you… No!'

I heard him telling someone he had to take this call; it was important.

'Yes. It's true. I heard a scream, just a few minutes ago, rushed round and found him. There was a motorcyclist. Anyway, the police will be here soon, but I thought you ought to know. Get back as soon as you can. Where are you?'

'I'm in Birmingham, arresting a suspect for that aggravated burglary I told you about. I'll be with you in an hour or so, tops. Don't touch anything. Don't go near the body – unless he's not dead.'

'Well I have and he is. Never mind. Just get here. Bye.'

I walked back into the kitchen where Catherine was filling a kettle. The young woman was seated with her elbows resting on the large wooden table. She had again covered her face with her hands and was visibly shivering. Catherine was just admonishing her to 'get a grip' on herself as I arrived.

'Tea?' the lady of the house enquired. The young woman

then stood up quickly and took over the arrangements, tears glistening on her cheeks.

'This is Matea,' Catherine explained, 'our nursing carer. From Croatia. She looks after my husband and Melissa, our daughter. You must be Dr Deane, are you?'

'Julia, please.'

'Your parents-in-law said how you visit them now on most weekends. I'm afraid I know them only slightly although they live so near. Our lives never seem to cross, I suppose.'

'Yes, they're really quite frail, so we come as often as we can at weekends. Well this weekend it's just me, David was coming, but got caught up in a heavy job, and well, I'm really sorry about...'

I trailed off, not knowing quite the right words when the corpse still lay just a few yards away.

I collected myself sufficiently to go on to say, 'I noticed a motorbike here. I followed it from the A38, on my way back from shopping at Aldi. I presume he, the rider, was the one who ... killed Mr Fletcher?'

'Yes,' said Matea, through sobs, 'I saw him. He was all black clothes, with a ...'

She curved her hands over her head, indicating a helmet.

'I open the door, and he was there... With a gun! Mr Fletcher, he was holding my arm. The man, he shoot and Mr Fletcher go "Ah!" and fall down.'

'What was the gun like, long or short?'

'It was a short gun with a long thing, like this,' Matea described in gestures an object which was obviously a silencer attached to the barrel. She was on the verge of hysteria so I suggested she said no more until the police arrived.

While she was clattering the mugs, and to save her yet further embarrassment, I turned into the hallway and studied the victim from a distance.

He was a white-haired man in his early seventies and still wearing a plaid dressing gown over striped pyjamas, although it was nearly midday. I remembered hearing from my mother-in-law how her neighbour was suffering badly from cancer and was bed-bound for much of the time. Matea must have been helping him walk when the murder occurred.

I felt strangely calm looking at death. Surprising, as I am usually a rather emotional person. It'll hit me later, I thought. Though, actually, it did not.

I returned to the kitchen and sat facing Matea at the sturdy wooden table. We all just drank our tea and said nothing, lost in thought. Matea snuffled into a series of paper handkerchieves, while Catherine stood almost motionless with her back to us, staring through the window.

Then the woman, now suddenly to be known as a widow, turned and went through the door into the room from which the barking of dogs had been heard earlier, closing it behind her. I could hear her talking to them, telling them to be good and behave themselves, and that their master would not be coming to see them, ever again. A couple of whimpers made me almost believe they had understood.

Time dragged while Matea sobbed and I mused on the randomness of sudden death and wondered how I would cope if someone took a shot at David like that. I always knew his work was dangerous and it was a real effort of will to control my anxiety whenever he returned late. This event brought home to me how easily death can be delivered, how anyone can be the victim of such a crime; even cancer-ridden retired neighbours in sleepy Gloucestershire villages.

Eventually vehicles scrunched up the drive and Catherine, with red, puffy eyes, returned to the kitchen, shutting the dogs in their own quarters.

The emergency services had arrived. We all stood at the window to watch while crime scene investigators zipped themselves into blue cover-alls. More police arrived, while ambulance men assembled a stretcher-trolley.

They all stood in groups talking with each other. The officers in blue cover-alls then walked purposefully towards the front door and out of our sight, while a uniformed officer and a scruffy-looking youth, led by a tiny woman in a cream coat and smart black trousers, came towards the house to our left, passing in front of us. Someone knocked on the side door.

Catherine sped into the gunroom to keep the dogs from physically welcoming the police officers and opened the outside door there, ushering the three people quickly into the kitchen away from the dogs.

The woman, a grim-faced short woman of about my age, flashed a small rectangle of black plastic with her ID and a badge.

She made the introductions,

'Hello everyone. I'm Detective Inspector Denise Walden from Gloucestershire Police and I'll be the Senior Investigating Officer on this case, and this,' pointing to the tousled-haired young man I had taken to be a teenager but must have been in his early twenties, 'is DC Hugh Evans. That's PC Thomas Ashley.'

We looked around at them and exchanged nods. DI Denise Walden then addressed Catherine,

'You must be Mrs Fletcher, who called us? I am very

sorry for your loss.' Perfunctory commiseration. Box ticked.

Then she turned towards the two of us and paused while Detective Constable Evans drew out a notebook and pen from the back pocket of his well-worn jeans.

'And you are?'

'I'm Julia Deane. With a final "e",' I added for the DC's benefit. 'I'm staying next door – with my in-laws. We come down from London nearly every weekend. My husband, David, is a DI in the Met.'

I did not say that to impress, but Denise Walden turned to catch the eye of her DC. I had the impression that she looked at me more attentively after that.

I felt the need to burble on.

'I teach there, London that is, at Queens College, part of London University.'

She remained impassive at that information, and turned to Matea.

'And I am Matea Pilić.'

Catherine noticed the DC floundering with the spelling.

'M-a-t-e-a P-i-l-i-c – with a little acute accent on the c', makes the sound ch, like in "cheese",' she interjected helpfully.

Matea continued, her cheeks now red from crying and distress.

'I am from Croatia. I have all the papers. I am legal. I live and work here, to care for Mr Fletcher and Melissa. She is not here, just now.'

'That's my daughter, Melissa. She's seventeen. James, her brother, has taken her to Riding for the Disabled at Cheltenham racecourse,' explained their mother.

'I was going also', Matea continued, 'but Mr Fletcher

# JULIA'S WORLD GOES WEST

say he want to walk in the garden as it is nice, sunny day. He is tired of always be in the bed. I help him so not to fall.'

'Have you contacted Melissa and James, Mrs Fletcher?'

'No, I thought I'd wait until they got home, after the body of their father has been taken away. I should hate Melissa to get such a shock. She's very disabled, brain injury. She goes to the National Star College during the week. And our son James is a student. He's at Worcester Uni. and lives here, at home. He'll be devastated. They both will.'

'What can you tell us about what happened?'

The young woman told them in faltering English how she and Mr Fletcher were in the hallway on the way to the kitchen and thence the garden through the gun room, when the front doorbell rang.

She relayed the same story she had told me, with the addition that the gunman had pushed up the darkly tinted visa of his helmet, presumably the better to see his target. The mouth was covered with a scarf, but she could see his eyes, nose and the top of a moustache. After the gun had gone off with 'phut' and Mr Fletcher had fallen, Matea remembered no more until I arrived. She thinks she may have screamed.

'I'll need you all come to the station this afternoon,' said DI Walden sternly. 'We'll use the local one at Tewkesbury. Just for you to give statements – to say what you said now. And maybe,' looking between Matea and me, 'you'll be able to recall some more details about that motorcyclist. And Mrs Fletcher, if you feel up to it, we'll need some background information about your husband – his friends and colleagues. Any enemies. That sort of thing. Meanwhile,' she added, looking towards the door to the gunroom, I'll ask you to use that door to go in and out, not the

9

front one. Council cleaners will be along shortly, after the CSIs have done their work. Sorry, Crime Scene Investigators, but you,' looking at me, 'probably know that already. We'll be back shortly to look around the house, if that's all right?'

Catherine nodded, then went back into the gunroom to control the dogs while the police followed her through it and left by the outside door. DI Walden turned back, having just remembered something. She called through to the kitchen, 'Oh, and we'll be sending an FLO to you shortly. Bye now.'

Catherine looked at me as the three police exited, and rolled her eyes heavenward.

'Family Liaison Officer', she snorted. 'God, they'll be foistering counseling on me next. Tell them I don't want any bloody policewoman holding my hand. I am a JP, you know.'

# Chapter 2

I HAD NOTHING TO TELL the DI about the Fletchers. My in-laws spoke little about any of their neighbours, despite having lived in the village for decades. Tony Deane's career was as a local solicitor, where discretion and confidentiality were the rule, and Terri had a contempt for the vulgarity of gossip.

Shame.

I prefer to call it 'taking an interest in people' and suspected their upmarket village would be rife with juicy scandal. The rambling ancient farm and manor-houses sprawling along the southern side of the long village road would each have their stories to tell of the doings of generations past and present.

The Fletchers' house, the most easterly in the village of Tredington, was from a different era, early 1930s rather than Jacobean, an anomalous white and blue Art Deco mansion, mercifully screened from the road by a dense row of mature conifers. When first built it was considered fashionably contemporary, all clean lines, light and spacious. It had been constructed on a generous parcel of land, the first plot for generations to be sold to a village incomer, an American magazine magnate. Terri had mentioned scandalous parties there before the war, but disappointingly would not elaborate.

Since then the house had passed through several hands, some quite famous, until the Fletchers had moved in a couple of decades ago. Other wealthy outsiders had bought up many of the village's more expensive properties and adapted them to all the modern criteria of comfort. Over the decades smaller developments of more modest houses had been built on the north side, but the village inhabitants still numbered around one hundred and thirty. A tiny community by today's standards. And normally, a peaceful one.

I told an attentive DI Walden and a bored-looking older uniformed officer all I could remember about the motorcyclist. I had driven behind him from the junction with the A38 until he turned in to the Fletchers' and I to the Deanes', but little had registered apart from it being a rare sight in the country to see people in leathers. I gave details of the scene that I found after hearing the scream. I was not detained long as had little to tell.

I returned to my in-laws' house after the police interview to find David seated in the kitchen at the large wooden table alongside his mother.

'Stop it, Mother! For goodness sake!'

He looked up as I walked in. I had seen that expression on him before – a mixture of embarrassment and exasperation.

Terri, the object of his annoyance, was clasping her boney hands around a mug of tea. Hers was a frail, tiny body made more fragile by severe osteoporosis combined with painful arthritis.

'Oh but, David,' she continued, oblivious of my arrival. 'Who's to say the gunman isn't roaming around the countryside looking for people to shoot? How do you know we won't be next?'

David looked up at me as he lay a comforting hand upon his mother's arm.

'No,' I mouthed silently.

The next day the mood in the car on the drive home was subdued. Approaching Oxford on the A40, I broke the silence, 'And the answer is still no.'

'What? You don't know what the question is yet!'

'Yes, I do. You're going to say that we need to move out here. Live with your mum and dad. Nurse them. Save them from mad gunmen. In the words of Maggie Thatcher, "No, no, no."'

***

The following weekend, back in Tredington, in the spacious first-floor bedroom where Tony was propped up with pillows and Terri about to administer her husband's night time supply of pills, glass of water in hand, David made the following announcement. Drum roll....

'Mum, Dad. Listen. Julia and I have something important to say. We've decided that we'll leave London, our work and flat…'

'And my mother,' I couldn't help interjecting – hoping they all realised the enormity of the sacrifice I was making on their account. David shot me a 'Who're you kidding?' look, and went on, 'And we'll move in here, with you. I'll see about a

13

transfer to Gloucestershire and Julia will look for another university post in the area, if there is one.'

Terri, for whom the expression of emotion was reserved for only major occurrences, was positively euphoric. She smiled. 'Oh, thank you, darling. David, how wonderful. And thank you too, Julia. That is most kind of you both.' She even seemed almost on the brink of tears. Not possible, but almost. 'I knew you wouldn't let us down. Oh, what a relief!'

Tony beamed at us and reached out his hand to clasp his wife's. She put down the water and held his hand, stroking it and murmuring, 'You see, Our Lady never lets us down. Our prayers have been answered.'

I looked at Terri and sighed inwardly. Can I really face living with this woman for the rest of her possibly long and increasingly frail life? What was it Frank Churchill says in *Emma*? 'There is safety in reserve but no attraction. One cannot love a reserved person.' Spot on, Jane.

Terri was only in her mid-seventies, and her own mother had lasted in a semi-invalided state for long beyond that age. Oh well, I shall have to start planning an escape route in case it does not work out. I promised David I would give it a go, at least for a year or so. Ho hum.

***

The Deane family home is one of those rambling black-timber-and-white-plaster farmhouses with extensions of weathered-red and others of white-washed brick. Parts of it date from the fourteenth century and each century has seen additions and alterations. In recent decades the Deanes overhauled it both structurally and decoratively, improving it in all aspects while maintaining its best ancient features.

Over the next couple of weekends we made arrangements for dividing the house. Apart from sharing the spacious kitchen with Terri, David and I would have the entire ground floor. The light and airy west-facing garden room, with double external doors, would become our bedroom. As well as connecting with the sitting room, a corridor led from the bedroom to the kitchen, taking in a shower room, a utility space for laundry, and a garden door. I was to use Tony's former library-study, and that left us with a easterly dining room and the capacious south-facing sitting room. I loved this grand chamber with its two wide sets of windows. A deep inglenook fireplace, crowned by a sixteenth-century carved mantel, faces the windows and is always ready for log fires to supplement the central heating. I had to admit it beat our cramped flat in Camden, and we would have a massive garden as well. It terms of accommodation, it was unbeatable.

The garden is mainly 'laid to lawn', in estate agent-speak, although near the road there is a walled-off kitchen garden, now largely abandoned to weeds. At some distance from the house there is a tennis court and further on, surrounded by trees and bushes, a fishpond. The garden is bordered by a long hedge separating it from the Fletcher's on the east, and by a dry stone wall on the south side, while a row of poplars marks the neighbours' acres on the west. Beyond the south wall a narrow bridle-lane separates the gardens from the field in which the Fletchers keep their horses. This mile-long lane is accessed by gates from the gardens of the houses which back onto it.

The Deanes possess a sit-on mower, stowed in one of the

former brick stables, a row of which lined the drive and backed along the main village road. These cobwebby sheds now housed cars and the bulkier garden equipment.

I could see David and I tussling over the key to the mower on summer evenings. It could be fun driving this oversized bumper car. Besides, I could see the  need for respite from having to make conversation with Terri. That had always made our weekend visits seem longer than they were.

Lacking a personal shop-steward, I had to negotiate hard before agreeing to this life-changing arrangement. The first concerned housework.

That would definitely not involve me. The Deanes had for some years employed Sue Roberts, a pleasant young and able single mother who lived locally, to come in three mornings a week to do the washing and cleaning. She also took away the damp laundry for ironing. That arrangement would continue. Definitely.

# Chapter 3

ON THE MONDAY following our announcement, David applied for an advertised detective inspector post in the Gloucestershire Constabulary and I handed in my notice at the university. The study of eighteenth-century literature at Queens would have to do without me from the end of the academic year.

I had competed my research into the eight plays of Fanny Burney and compiled the notes into explanatory essays and footnotes for a two-volume edition of all of them. This would be the first published for twenty years and incorporated as much of the latest scholarship as I could find. It had been fascinating and delightful work, but exhausting. I had been obliged to make time for this while teaching undergraduates and postgrads and coping with the ridiculous obligatory amount of bureaucratic paperwork. Now was as good a time as any to take a break.

I could have opted for a year's sabbatical, and then resigned, but resisted the temptation. Instead I called Sarah Wells, a close friend during my student days and with whom I had kept in touch. She had gone into publishing, becoming a commissioning editor for the firm which was handling my book on the plays. We met in a quiet pub and I called in a favour.

'You know you once asked if I could write a book for the general market about the Burney family – all of them, including Fanny's step-sister Elizabeth Meeke? Well, is that offer still open? I'm asking because I'll soon be out of a job, long story, and will at last have the time to write it.'

Sarah smiled and agreed, 'I'll have to speak to my colleagues. They like your edition of the plays, and I'm sure they'll go for a general one about the whole family. It'll tap in to the growing market of interest in the Burney tribe.'

She paused, then hit me with the condition, 'I'd like it by summer of next year, ready for the big Burney conference in the United States. Your book of the plays is already going to it. I'm fixing up your talk to the conference – you will make it, won't you?'

That was a tight deadline – just one year in which to do all the reading necessary, then to write the book and to have it published and ready. At least with its wide scope and aiming at a general or undergraduate readership, to  whom the Burneys are still largely unknown, I did not need to go into too much original research. More broad brushstroke than fine detail.

I relished the challenge. The financial rewards would be minimal, but work on such a subject would be a pleasure, and ultimately not harm my career. There was no likelihood of a university post in the West of England becoming available for the next academic year, so writing would fill the gap nicely.

David's transfer to Gloucestershire Constabulary was painless, but he just scraped in before a freeze on recruitment was introduced. The police there had experienced an upsurge in the murder rate over the past few years and were looking for a detective inspector with specialist experience of serious crimes to join the new three forces Brunel Major Crime Collaboration. This pooled the resources of the murder squads from Gloucestershire, Wiltshire, and Avon and Somerset, and Gloucestershire had only recently joined the other two forces. David's record at the Met ticked all the boxes.

As soon as he passed the interviews and health and fitness tests (which had caused him a few sleepless nights and a sudden increase in gym attendance), his transfer was assured. The Met released him reluctantly, but without obstruction, on compassionate grounds.

I congratulated him, while uncorking a bottle of Prosecco.

'Oh, don't gush. They're crying out for DIs. Who wants to work all the hours under the sun for no extra pay? It's all right for uniform, and juniors in the department. They can claim overtime and make thousands that way. I can't.'

David was not usually given to negative thinking. His was a steady temperament, not given to the highs and lows of which I was subject. Sometimes I envied his equanimity. It is less exhausting than bouts of emotion and leads to calmer judgments.

At other times I felt sorry that he could not experience the intensity of joy in which I could delight, even though they were balanced by occasional and unbidden blue moods. At least, I told myself, I can feel more fully alive, even though I submit to a tendency to act too compulsively, not a helpful trait in a policeman, or allow people or incidents to upset me unduly. We are a good match. We balance each other.

'Don't worry, I'm sure the different experience will be good for your career.' I passed him his glass and moved closer, gently hooking my hand behind his neck. He drew back a step and shook my hand away.

'Huh! It's hardly promotion, a sideways step, no more. In fact,' he added ruefully, 'a drop in actual pay as I'll lose the London weighting.'

'Still, you won't have to pay rent.' There had to be a bright side. I was doing my best.

'True,' he admitted. 'And the daily commute will be a doddle. Straight down the M5 and the Gloucestershire HQ is just off the motorway, south of Gloucester.'

He cheered up at the thought. After all, this was his idea. He was the one who wanted to uproot us both and settle us here in the back of beyond. I felt slighted by his rejection of my gesture. A while back he would have welcomed and responded to it. I turned and took my glass into the sitting room. My resentment simmered while I sipped. I felt that he owed me. I was offering to give up everything for his benefit and for the sake of his parents.

I began to find reasons for his chill. Perhaps he was nervous at starting in a new post. Maybe the responsibility of family caring and work would be too much. Perhaps he realised he had so much to make up to me. I pondered the ways he would no doubt deliver the forms of compensation – greater attentiveness, greater warmth.... I began to smile inwardly. Once we were settled, this could herald a new phase of our ten-year-old marriage. Maybe we could even start a family, before time ran out.

Time.

Time would tell.

I loved David. I loved his nature and, yes, his looks. Even features, calm blue eyes and short auburn hair that would have been a mass of curls had it been allowed to grow. His smile had the effect of making me feel valued, appreciated.

There are some people, David included, for whose good opinion of me I had a deep and hungry need, just as there were some teachers at school whom I sought most to impress. It is something about their possession of natural authority, and their expectations of excellence or at least high standards. Experts in any subject always fascinate and attract me. Being favoured by a rare smile, or a confidence, or a comment of approval from such a person would cause me to feel a physical warmth of pleasure. I would mentally hug myself in sheer joy.

Maybe my not knowing my father lies at the root. I am not a psychologist, but I suspect that plays a part. As well as being brought up by someone who drove themselves to constant self-improvement; my Nana Ivy – always questioning, assessing, discerning. Never settling for ready-made opinions or media manipulations. I could not have been raised by any better parent. She was poor, widowed and lacked formal education beyond her mid-teens, but was wise, knowledgable and loving. She protected me from the sense of having been abandoned by my mother, who had preferred living communally with a lot of fellow ageing hippies on a near-derelict farm in north Wales, to motherhood. Nana Ivy had allowed me the freedom to travel, had encouraged my school endeavours, and had left it to me to make such choices as to what to study and what to do with my life. She had been so proud of my Cambridge scholarship, something that would have been unheard of in her younger days to someone of her background. Then at college I met David, almost straight away, and we had never been apart since.

David's good opinion of me I still valued, even after ten years of marriage, and even though there were aspects of him that irritated or annoyed. But I had learned to take those on board as the price to pay for all his other, more admirable, qualities.

Even David's slightly obsessive neatness I tolerated as a necessary corrective to my tendency to create instant mess. In our small, cramped London flat this was a continual cause of potential friction. I absolutely needed to spread papers and books around every surface, including large tracts of floor space, when I worked at home. His silent disapproval ensured that I at least made a gesture of clearing some of them away. I understood and even appreciated that. We would then enjoy an hour or two of evening relaxation. Television provided most of that, with a glass or two of wine or whisky.

Often he returned home too late and on those occasions I might visit my mother, whose television I could hear blaring away from the flat below ours most of the evening. I would have to be feeling really lonely and neglected to make those visits, but there were times when even her company was better than nothing.

Her husband, our respectable neighbour Ronald who had recently and astonishingly found in my mother a suitable companion for life, bore his new situation well, and seemed actually to be enjoying her company.

That all would change now. No work-place for me other than home, no mother to call on. But a wonderfully spacious study I could keep permanently untidy. Not untidy, exactly.

'Creative clutter', is how my ever-understanding Nana Ivy, would call it. What a love.

# Chapter 4

THE MURDER HAD TAKEN place in mid-March, and David reported for his first day at Prism House, Gloucestershire police's shiny new headquarters at Quedgeley, in June. I gave my notice in early at the university but had to wait until the end of August before being released, after marking and assessing the examination resit papers that were taken then.

In those summer months of June and July I had time during the week to enjoy living in the Camden flat on my own. Without David I could spread my work around the sitting room, piled up on the sofa, fanned out on the floor, organised on the window ledges. And leave them there like that.

Only viewers for the flat interrupted this idyll. I advertised widely for someone who would be acceptable to the landlord, to whom to assign the tenancy.

Several viewers left saying 'Thank you for your time', but their faces meant, 'Forget it.' I had cleared up for nothing.

Then Louisa, a younger colleague in the English department, mentioned that she would be keen to move in with her new partner. Problem solved.

Work was intense as the vacation approached. I had some minor alterations to make to the book of Burney plays – a sharp-eyed editor had noticed details that I had missed. Then the students needed me to mark papers and provide references, while the faculty wanted help with setting and marking examinations. Postgrad students, part way through their theses, were reluctant to let me go and transfer to other supervisors. I could not blame them, but cannot be chained to them either.

I helped with the interviews for my replacement and wished the young Canadian woman well who was given the post. She had recently completed her doctorate at the prestigious Burney Centre at McGill University, Montreal. Her thesis was on the use of humour in Frances Burney's plays (North Americans tend to avoid the name 'Fanny') and we had corresponded frequently over my work on the plays. She would be fine. Even, I begrudgingly admitted to myself, better than me.

David meanwhile spent his spare time preparing our quarters in Tredington. At the weekends we went happily shopping in Cheltenham for furniture and furnishings. I had to admit that Terri possessed excellent taste, so that the house was already rather beautifully appointed. It was difficult to find ways of making it feel really like our own home, so we bought a new television and other, more trivial items, and rearranged the furniture. Tony's study was cleared of his books, some of which were stored in a spare bedroom, and others went to local charity shops.

On the Friday afternoon drive after work, joining the London weekend exodus to the West along the M4, I would listen to my favourite classical music CDs or the radio, sometimes needing to switch on the local traffic bulletins channels. By the time I turned off at Swindon to follow A419 and 417 roads, I would feel the cares of work fall away behind me and begin to anticipate a weekend of countryside relaxation. The route took me past Cirencester and I would cut up the M5 to Tewkesbury, before dropping back to the village of Tredington. By the time I arrived the sheer beauty of the early summer countryside would have cosseted me in delight.

Gloucestershire is a county of exceptional beauty, with its undulating hills and still-unspoilt villages of old Cotswold stone buildings blending unobtrusively into the lush leafy landscape. Over the years of visiting the senior Deanes, we would take walks down country lanes or over Cleeve hill, visit the Pittville Park in Cheltenham with its stately neo-classical Pump Room, and amble along the riverbank in Tewkesbury. There was always much to see, to explore, to visit, and to give hope of happy days to come.

It was with mixed feelings therefore that I handed over the keys of the flat which had been our first and only home together. My mother, who always wanted to be known by her name Helena (pronounced *Heleena*), made a show of maternal regret by throwing her arms around me.

'I'll miss you, lovey. I've not seen as much of you as I'd've liked, but it was always a comfort knowing you were just upstairs. You and David will always be welcome back to visit, you know. Just say, and Ronald and I'll be ever so happy.'

I found it quite easy to break away from her embraces and drive off to my new life.

How was I to know that more tragedy lay ahead?

# Chapter 5

BACK IN THE SPRING, and the Saturday after Ian Fletcher's murder, David and I were once again weekending in the Deanes' home. Catherine Fletcher telephoned and asked me to go round for coffee and to meet someone. I was just at the point of breadmaking when I had to leave the dough to rise, so happily accepted, scrubbed my doughy hands, and was round there in a matter of minutes. Catherine had watched my approach and was at the front door ready for me.

'Come in and meet Jessica,' she said, rolling her eyes with exaggerated annoyance.

I followed her into the kitchen, where a young blond woman sat at the table, notebook open in front of her and a mug of coffee beside it. She smiled in a cold, formal way, and allowed Catherine to introduce her.

'This is DC Jessica Smy, our Family Liaison Officer. Jessica, this is my neighbours' daughter-in-law, Dr Julia Deane. She was here just after the murder. Helped your DI with her investigation, and was very helpful to me when it happened.'

DI Walden had mentioned sending out an FLO, but I had the impression she would be a motherly older woman. This one was mid-twenties, thin and slight, with darting brown eyes and hair bottle-blonded with dark roots, pulled back into a ponytail.

'Pleased to meet you.' She did not look it. 'I'll be going now then, Catherine. Unless Dr Deane has remembered anything about the murder of Mr Fletcher that she hasn't told anyone about yet?'

I shook my head. I'm not so stupid that I would sit on anything that could be relevant. I tried to cover a momentary vexation with a watery smile. She handed me a business card with her contact details on, 'In case anything comes to mind', she explained.

Catherine took her through to the front door while I settled on one of the chairs at the kitchen table.

'Well, Julia. What do you think of that? What do I need with an FLO I ask you! And she's only really here to see if she can jog my memory. A sort of spy in the house! Puh!'

I acquiesced with a nod and a smile. She continued, still standing by the door to the corridor that led to the front door.

'Anyway, I wanted you to meet her, but also, really, to say thank you for the enormous help you were last week, when Ian was killed, and to let you know that the funeral is on Tuesday, if you can make it. They released the body on Thursday after the post mortem, so I've arranged the service for 11 o'clock at the church across the road, then back here while I go to the crematorium with James.'

I made a mental note, while she went on,

'It would be too much for Melissa, so Matea – you met Matea, the young Croatian help, of course you have – will come back with Melissa here and entertain the guests. Please let Mr and Mrs Deane know. They will be more than welcome. I'm not expecting many people. Keeping it fairly low-key. Don't want a fuss.'

'I'm not able to take the time off, but I'll pass on the message to Terri and Tony…'.

Any further discussion was cut off by the sudden arrival, from the room beyond the kitchen, of a projectile golden spaniel, followed more sedately by two large black Labradors.

The spaniel shot across the expanse of kitchen towards me. Then he alternated between stretching up to lick my face, front paws patting my arms while he hopped excitedly on back legs, or else he took to revolving in rapid circles, energetically wagging his whole back quarters and yapping with excitement. The two larger more placid dogs duly sniffed hard around my legs and licked my outstretched hands.

'Dogs, no! Captain, behave yourself! Charlie, Captain, Cracker, out at once. Into your room. Not a sound.'

Their mistress gestured towards the door to the room from which they had come, and the dogs dutifully filed out, the spaniel casting me loving backward glances.

'So sorry about that. They are such a handful. Need more exercise, that's what.'

She closed the door into the dogs' room, which I learnt she called, pretentiously I thought, the 'gun room', and proffered a filter jug of coffee at me. I nodded and she filled two mugs, adding milk. She handed me one and sat down at the table.

'They live in the gun room, as a rule. But I do allow them into the kitchen while I'm working here.' She went on, 'I really am most terribly glad you came when you did last week. What a simply awful business.'

I made the appropriate murmur of consent.

She paused, looking wistful. 'I don't know what came over me, stunned I suppose, but I couldn't think of what to do until you called to us to telephone the police.'

I waved away her gratitude and let her carry on talking, as she obviously wanted to do.

'What you must think of me I cannot imagine. Of course, I was deeply affected by it, still am really, but didn't want to show it in front of Matea. Really, that girl has no control over her emotions. She carried on blubbing for hours. You'd think he'd been her husband, not mine!'

She then leaned over towards me confidentially, 'Well, he had a soft spot for her, but even apart from his illness, he wouldn't have got far with that one. She told me once that she was saving herself up for marriage. Quite a novelty these days, especially when you see some of the girls who come before me on the bench. Sex, drugs and rock'n'roll – you know the sort. It's the boys I feel sorry for these days. Still, mustn't bore you with all that. I see you're baking.'

My floury sweater told her that, plus stubborn morsels of dough on my hands.

'Well done you. So many people these days just buy their stuff factory made. Good to see some real food being prepared. Anyway, tell me. Are you moving in here? There's some talk in the village about that.'

29

I told her of our plans, that David was joining the local police and I would be writing a book once I'd given up lecturing.

'Really?' she said with faint curiosity. 'What's the book about?'

'Oh, the various members of the eighteenth-century Burney family. There are a few books about Dr Charles, the father and musicologist, and Fanny, the novelist, playwight and journal-keeper, but nothing in just one book so far accounting for all the members – and there were so many of them, all fascinating and brilliant in their own spheres.'

I could see I had lost her. Her eyes had glazed after the first few words. 'Do you read, er, novels?' I ventured.

'Heavens, no!' she shuddered. 'No time for that! I'm far too busy. As I say, I've been a local magistrate for some years, a JP, and run the garden club in the village, as well as ride. Introduced my husband to riding and shooting. Lots of rabbits around here, you know. Hunting became his passion. Have you seen our horses? They live in the field off the lane at the back of these houses. The  stables are just behind your in-laws' garden. Over there.' She waved towards the south. 'Do you ride?'

As riding is not an essential urban pursuit, I just shook my head, adding, 'No, I work full time. I'm a lecturer at Queen's College, in Kingsway, London. You know, off the Strand.'

'London! I never go near the place, if I can. All that noisy traffic, the fumes, and people rushing about! Not my scene at all. I'm a countrywoman, born and bred. Born locally, Cropthorne, just over the border in Worcestershire, and went to school here, day girl at the Ladies College.'

'Ah, yes. The famous Cheltenham Ladies' College'

She went on, 'My husband though, he was a Londoner.'

She paused, reflectively. 'Ian lived and worked in London most of his life  until he came to Cheltenham. He was in MI5 when we met. Was over here for a conference with GCHQ. We married and… well, obviously, I wouldn't go to London, so he got transferred to GCHQ. We eventually moved to this village, about fifteen years ago when the children were small.'

'MI5, really? The spy world. Spooks! How exciting!' I gamely ventured. Knowledge of Catherine's pursuance of blood sports had expunged any fondness or sympathy I might have felt for her. I was forcing myself to be sociable.

'Exciting? Not really,' she replied. 'I worked there too, in GCHQ. Dull stuff really. Clerical. Can't go into it, of course. Anyway, I gave it up when the children came along.'

'By train?' I felt like saying. I am such a child.

'Ian stayed in the service until he retired. Much quieter than his MI5 work. That was really quite dangerous. Involved him in going out to Northern Ireland quite a lot during the Troubles. However, he didn't have long to enjoy his retirement, did he? Ironic really, killing him when he was going to die soon anyway, the doctors say.'

'Really, his cancer was that bad?'

'Oh yes, that's why we got Matea from an agency in Cheltenham. We had a couple of these foreign girls before her, more au pairs than nurses, young unqualified carers, originally just to take care of our daughter Melissa. She had tutors as well, of course, but really she needed looking after constantly.'

She stood up and rinsed her coffee mug under the tap.

'I'm not sure what we'll do with Matea now that she doesn't have Ian to look after. She's a nurse more than an au pair. We needed a nurse when Ian's cancer got worse.'

'How badly brain-damaged is Melissa?' I asked.

'Oh, quite seriously. She cannot speak much, just odd words, and finds walking tiring as she moves so awkwardly. When Melissa is home Matea is an enormous help. They get on so well together. James is also really good with his sister. He takes the leading rein when she's on her pony. He also takes her to the Riding for the Disabled. They have a centre down at the racecourse. Her old pony Peanut is still in the field behind us, but she doesn't like to ride Peanut any more without help. James is such a good boy, endless patience with her.'

'How did she become brain-damaged?' I asked.

'She had an accident a few years ago, when she was just twelve. Her father took her to the Boxing Day hunt, the Cotswold Farmers. You know, their hounds are kenneled just down the lane opposite. Frightful noise they make sometimes!'

I had heard the distant barking and howling of several dogs. Now I understood why.

Catherine resumed her seat at the table.

'Ian and I used to enjoy riding to hounds, even after the wretched ban on chasing foxes, but Melissa wasn't ready. She had not taken to riding as a child – more the ballet and tutus, that sort of thing. Then just a couple of months earlier she took it up when we gave her this new pony Peanut. But she was still very much a novice.

Anyway, Ian took her with him. The foolish man. I wasn't there, been collecting James from friends of his where he'd been spending Christmas. I wouldn't have allowed her to go, not actual hunting, not in all that mud. The ground was far too soft. Her pony sank in it and didn't make the jump. Melissa fell, hitting her head on a boulder. The helmet was useless; it didn't protect her at all. She was in a coma for three weeks; we thought she'd not recover. She did, but not completely. She now needs constant attention, hence Matea. However, things are looking up for her now. Now she's seventeen she goes to the Star.'

'Sorry, what?'

'Oh, it's a quite wonderful place, just south of Cheltenham. National Star College. Sort of Further Education place, prepares young disabled adults for making the most of their lives. Those who can work are taught a skill, others simply how to survive. Melissa is one of those. She goes in as a day student, loves it. I'm a huge fan of the place. Take you to see it sometime.'

'Yes, thanks. You said to the DI that James was a student?'

'Oh James. Yes, he's studying maths and business something-or-other. Doing all right. I have to admit, he's a young man we're – I'm – so very proud of. Did well at school, Malvern. Was offered a place at Cambridge, but we felt he'd be better off living at home, so he's at Worcester University and drives in each day.'

My mind wandered as I considered how the good son James must have felt at being deprived of his place at Cambridge. I would have seethed. Those years I spent there were the best of my life. I had left home. It was where I had met David. Catherine's screening him from the world could not be good for him. The words of a passage I had read only that morning in Fanny Burney's *Evelina*, surfaced. I had thought it admirably expressed;

'When young people are too rigidly sequestered from [the world], their lively and romantic imaginations paint

33

it to them as a paradise of which they have been beguiled; but when they are shown it properly, and in due time, they see it such as it really is, equally shared by pain and pleasure, hope and disappointment.'

I then came to, to hear Catherine still speaking, 'He is so kind and patient with Melissa. I have to admit I don't give her the time I should. But I'm so busy. It's simply terrible. The Department of Justice keeps sending masses of paperwork every week. I have to plough through it all, takes hours. Still, it's all the penalty of putting something back into the community.'

I could imagine her on the bench. Heaven help the poor defendants. She changed the subject, remembering her manners.

'How is Mrs Deane, Theresa, isn't it? Or Terri, is that what you call her? I don't see much of her these days. And Anthony – still having problems with his heart?'

After waiting for me to make the appropriate comments on their health, she rose and announced,

'Well, now, you'd best get back. The dough will spoil if it's neglected! Thank you so much for coming, and again for having helped out when Ian was killed. I do hope they find the brute soon.'

She collected my coffee mug and made for the sink, then turned to add, 'Anyway, give my best wishes to Mr and Mrs Deane, and do pop round for a chat next time you're visiting. And of course, if I can help in any way when you move in, just let me know.'

I felt I'd been dismissed, if very politely. I walked back wondering whether I could ever be friends with the woman.

'I must try to get to know her better', I told myself

virtuously. 'And maybe I might even get to like her.'
      Doubtful.

# Chapter 6

'YOU'VE BEEN OUT?' That was Terri, shuffling into the kitchen, leaning heavily on her walking stick. She often made the journey from her first floor quarters in search of a cup of coffee or tea, although was quite capable of making one herself upstairs. She said she preferred company while her husband spent long daytime hours asleep. Trouble is, that company consisted solely of me. David was usually out in the garden, or running ,errands, or at his computer in his father's study. Anywhere but the kitchen.

'I've been at your neighbour's, Catherine Fletcher,' I answered, scrubbing stubborn dough out of the mixing bowl. 'She asked me to go round there to thank me for helping when her husband was shot. Oh, and to invite you to the funeral on Tuesday; church across the road at eleven, then back to the house.'

'Hum,' she uttered, through pursed lips. 'I might make the church part; but not the house. She didn't exactly overdo the help for me when Tony had his heart attack. She's only been here a couple of times. Not that I want her here, with her muddy shoes and her wretched dogs. She's too busy being a do-gooder to do anybody any actual good, if you ask me.'

'She seems OK,' I offered magnanimously. 'Have you seen her daughter – the brain-damaged girl?'

'Yes, occasionally, in the village. Along with that foreign girl who looks after her. Poor Melissa, I remember when she was such a bright and pretty little girl, before the accident. Well, that's what comes of all that hunting and shooting. Did you hear the dogs last night? Why she needs a spaniel as well as two great Labradors, I can't imagine! All that mud and smell!'

I offered to make Terri some tea, and she hobbled back upstairs towards her sitting room.

A few weekends later, when I was back at the house and while David was doing the supermarket run, I received another call from Catherine. She had an idea she wanted to share. This time I invited her round to the Deanes' to discuss it. She turned up, with the three dogs in tow, and I ushered them all into the kitchen. The three dogs made short work of stray crumbs on the floor, and took it in turns to slurp from the bowl of water I put down for them.

'How about,' Catherine broached, coffee mug in hand, 'your having Matea here during the day when Melissa is at college? Not during the summer holidays, of course. She could come over here after she's seen to Melissa. Once she's up and out on the college bus, Matea could deal with the Deanes in the daytime, and come back to us when Melissa is home in the evening and overnight. That way you get care for your in-laws and I have the girl out from under my feet during the day.'

I was struck by the utter brilliance of the notion. Tony and Terri would have company during the day, to fetch and carry, and see that they took their medication, and prepare their lunch.

My readiness to accept was not through pure altruism. I had been worrying about how I could write my book when at the constant  beck and call of the senior Deanes. I knew the housework was largely taken care of by Sue Roberts, but sewing needles required threading, dropped balls of wool retrieving, endless teas being made and the medicine routines required servicing. All would lead to my being chained to the house and my train of thought interrupted throughout the day.

I thanked her profusely, while patting and stroking her attentive canines.

'Is Matea herself OK with it?'

'Oh, she's fine about it,' Catherine said with assurance. 'She wants to be useful, and now that Ian is no longer here, she is keen to care for your people. She does have some nursing training and is a willing runaround.'

My neighbour drank her coffee and waved away a proffered biscuit.

'Also,' she added, leaning forward confidentially, 'strictly between us, you know, James is rather struck with her. So I feel that the less they see of each other, the better. We had a frightful row the other day when I suggested we could get rid of her altogether now the reason for much of her work has gone. I must admit it was his idea that she worked for you. He insists she is brilliant with Melissa, which I grant you is so, and Melissa dotes on her. I just wish she and James weren't quite so chummy.'

'She seems a nice girl.'

'Oh, nice, yes. Nice enough. She'll be excellent for your people; a good and thoughtful carer. But not the right partner for James. He is barely twenty yet and I have plans for him that don't involve some little foreign domestic! Anyway, if she's no good, you can always shove her back!'

To my relief, David was happy to accept the deal, and his parents needed little persuasion. They relished the thought of constant attention.

David telephoned the number Catherine left with me for Nikos Konstantinou, the CEO of the Cheltenham agency through which Matea was employed. The Greek Cypriot businessman accepted the terms readily. The cost for us was not high, and everyone seemed to like the girl already, so all was in place for the start of the Autumn term when Melissa would return to college.

David and I spent the summer working, I at college and the flat, he in his new cop shop in Gloucester. By the end of August I was exhausted and looking forward not to having to worry about Queen's College work any longer. I felt then that if I never set foot in a university again, that would be fine by me. Packing and moving took place over several weekends. It was a chore but at least I found all sorts of things I had forgotten about or thought were lost.

I moved in, with the rest of my clutter from the flat, on 1st September 2016. Matea began working for us two weeks after that, on the day Melissa started the new term at the National Star College.

David, now confident his parents were being well looked after, went off to work each day with a spring in his step. He worked late, and complained little. The team around him, he told me, was young and intelligent, eager to show this ex-Met copper how efficient a rural police service could be. The new collaborative project of pooled resources between three rural police services appeared to be working, and David's rich experience was valued. The case of the murder of Ian Fletcher was transferred to him from DI Walden as soon as he arrived. Denise Walden was apparently relieved to be rid of being the Senior Investigating Officer on it. She preferred to concentrate on cases of domestic abuse and crimes against women.

'That's how she wants to make her name,' my spouse explained as I voiced, rather heatedly, the complaint that yet another woman was being passed over for the sake of a man. 'Honestly, she wanted out. There are some high-profile wife-battering cases she wants to be involved with. She really does.'

One night in late summer, the weather stifling and neither of us managing sleep, I asked David how the Fletcher investigation was going.

'Slowly. We're working on the theory that the killer was somehow connected with Fletcher's MI5 job in Northern Ireland during the Troubles. We think it more than likely it was an IRA man getting his own back, or a Unionist chap thinking he'd been betrayed. One line is that the agents MI5 co-opted, willing or otherwise, were left rather high and dry after the Good Friday agreement in 1998. Some of them got it in the neck – or literally, the head – in revenge attacks. We know some of them held grudges against their London masters. Maybe one of them did it. We don't know yet.'

'What if..?'

'Oh, here we go!'

'No, listen. What if he wasn't the target at all?'

'We've thought of that.'

'Well, what if *she* was – maybe someone she had come up against as a JP?'

'Hardly likely. It would more likely be a judge in the criminal court than a humble JP.'

'There's not much humble about her! Or, worse for us…What if it was your father, as an ex-solicitor who was the target and the gunman went to the wrong house? Or even you! One of your London gangland killers thinking all houses in the country look the same!'

'Oh shut up, Julia! You're sounding like my mother. She thinks it was a random shooting and the killer just has a grudge against rich people in the countryside, and that we'll be next!'

I turned over to face away from him, and whereas at one time David would have tried to coax me out of my sulk, he simply turned away too and was soon snoring. I hated him sometimes.

*\*\*\**

I found it easy at first to adapt to country life, partly because there was so much to do in gathering my material for the book of the Burneys. I missed the gossip of colleagues and the youthful ebullience of postgrad students, but generally I was surviving rather better than I thought I would in this non-urban environment. After all, the Gloucestershire countryside has different aspects of beauty in all seasons, and when October arrived with sunshine and warmth, I found much pleasure in taking a book into the garden, or strolling along the bridlepath behind the gardens, talking to the curious horses who would walk alongside on their side of the hedge.

After David left home I would shower and then slouch along to the kitchen, waking myself up with a mug of freshly ground coffee. Then I'd take the in-laws their breakfast on trays and see that they took their morning medication.

After that, knowing that Matea was on her way, I could concentrate on work. Mostly I sat at the large mahogany desk in what was Tony's study, and wrote notes and read from books, journals, and internet resources on the laptop. Sometimes, when there was a lot of straight reading to do, I would take the material into the sitting room and sink into a comfortable chair sideways to the light. My first tasks were to assemble what I needed, and go through some of the wads of papers I had brought from the university to sort out the apposite from the redundant.

I discovered there was a bus service that left Cheltenham every morning for Oxford, with the return service in the evening. On the first trip I joined the University's Bodleian library and thereafter tried to make the journey to it once or twice a week. I chose to work in the famous small circular and domed Radcliffe Camera, the eighteenth-century neoclassical reading room standing in a cobbled square behind the main library, and where most of the English literature books are shelved that are not in the store. It appealed strongly to the romantic in me, and somehow the atmosphere, being surrounded by youthful scholars tapping away silently on their laptops, helped me to keep my mind on the task. Not that I needed much encouragement. The Burney tribe deserved whole books to themselves individually, and it became a real effort to know how to trim the material to fit one volume.

Apart from Thursdays, Matea's day off – half of which she spent taking the English lessons arranged by her agency – she arrived each day around nine and left at five. She performed her light household duties with a delightful cheerfulness, and soon was close friends with Sue Roberts. They worked together as a team, each trying to save the other from unnecessary effort. Matea prepared lunch for Terri and Tony, and for me when I was at home, and left behind a cold collation for the evening.

David lunched at work and then raided the fridge at whatever time he returned in the evening. Tony and Terri took their meals in Tony's bed-sitting room, where there was a small dining table. I ate in the kitchen with Matea and got to know the young woman who had cried on my shoulder just a few months previously.

'What's Mrs Fletcher like to work with?' I asked one day as we were sharing a vegetarian bolognese in the kitchen.

'Oh she is fine. I not speak much with her as she is

always very busy. I think she love her daughter but she not like to be much with sick people. Mr Fletcher and Melissa. Not much time with them.'

That was what I had already assumed. Not that I am Florence Nightingale. But Matea, thank goodness, had the patient kindly nature required for the demands of caring. She had trained in basic nursing while at school, and decided to see some more of the world before settling down. She reminded me of some of the students I had left behind. I thought about Toya and Abigail, Vanessa and poor dead Tom. Their lives were filled with book-learning but also with romance and the ups and downs of relationships.

I looked at this tall, slender young girl with her long shining hair, ready smile and black laughing eyes and caught myself asking aloud whether she had a boyfriend. Unforgivable cheek.

'Oh, no. Nothing serious!' She gave a quick, forgiving laugh, then frowned.

'There is a boy from my neighbourhood, in Dubrovnik. Luka wants to marry me, but I don't want to be with him. His parents are friends of my family and they all think he is good for me. But I don't like him! No, that is not right. I like him OK, but I do not want to be his wife. It will be like in prison! He has ideas that are very old fashioned of how woman must be. I don't want that!'

I agreed that in the 21$^{st}$ century we women do not want to be shackled by men. Once started on the subject of boyfriends, she was on a roll.

'Also there is a Serbian boy in my English school. Zivko. He likes me too, but is a horrible man! He follows me everywhere. Always he asks, "Come with me. Be my woman. Why not you come with me?".'

Then she blushed, and chuckled shyly, 'No, I like James, the brother of Melissa, and I think he likes me. He is a good boy, very funny, and loves his sister very much. He says he respects me, that I am different from other girls. And … he is very handsome!'

She said that last with an engaging giggle. I was intrigued. James seemed a rare youth – possibly something of a Mummy's boy (I am so quick to judge) yet kind to his sister and with the looks and personality to attract the affection of this delightful young woman. I had seen him briefly in his two-tone Mini-Cooper around the village, and in and out of his drive, but had yet to meet him. I could hardly wait.

.

# Chapter 7

'DAVID…?'

'Mmmm?' '

'Well?'

'Well, what?'

'You know.'

'Oh, come on. I've had a hard day.'

'Never stopped you before!'

'Yeah, well, we've got Mum and Dad just upstairs don't forget. And you know what you're like! Can't do it exactly quietly, can you?'

'So? We're married, aren't we?'

'Yeah, well. Maybe tomorrow. G'night.'

***

By the time October passed, we were finding little niggles

in each other's behaviour, little irritants that sometimes turned into raging rows. We had never been so edgy and disagreeable with each other before.

'Let's go away,' I suggested after one particularly heated exchange. 'Take some bloody time off work once in a while, and let's get out of here. Come on, just for a night, at least.'

'Don't blame being here,' he retorted unreasonably. 'Just because you're extra moody these days. You're not..?'

'No, fat chance!'

'Anyway, how will Mum and Dad cope overnight? What if Dad needs help going to the bathroom?'

Bother! He was right, but I was feeling trapped. It was as if a holiday had ended, a newness of things losing its gloss. My own company for hours on end was not as engaging as I had imagined. Even annoying interruptions by friendly or enquiring colleagues would have been welcome now. Anything that could link me to the real world. Two elderly invalids and one foreign Miss, just did not stimulate enough. And David was leaving earlier and returning later than ever before. I hardly saw him, and when it did there was a loss of warmth, a sparkle was going. Was it me?

Bloody hell, I thought. We are a stone's throw from quaint and bustling Tewkesbury. We could at least go to a film or show at the Roses Theatre. And, crikey, Cheltenham is on the doorstep. Right. I decided. I shall look into what is going on in the area. There's bound to be one festival or other for starters. I don't have to wait for David to be free, I'll start making a life for myself here or I'll go daft.

I was soon to have more mental stimulation that I

wanted, but whoever knows what is around the corner?

\*\*\*

I considered, in my more generous moments, that David was under increasing pressure at work. After all, he seemed no nearer to solving the Ian Fletcher murder case. So I began to try my best not to add to his stress when he eventually returned home at night. I felt I was turning into a 1950s housewife, soothing the troubled brow of the master of the house. I ensured there were no papers or books spilling over surfaces in the kitchen and sitting room, that there was always something in the fridge for him to eat whatever time he returned, and that there was always a bottle of wine opened. That was never a problem. But even as a Stepford wife, I seemed no longer to delight him as I once did. Perhaps I was becoming too boring, my conversation too banal, too non-metropolitan.

\*\*\*

Nearly eight months had passed since the Fletcher murder, and questions were being asked in the local media about how effective the police reorganisation was proving. The joint three-counties murder squad was being accused of inefficiency and a local MP brought up a question about it in the House of Commons. The regional TV channels, keen to exploit the human interest of this news story, began to make outrageous speculations about the Fletcher murder, linking the case to one several years before of another MI5/GCHQ man found dead in a sports bag in his bath.

Reporters were sometimes spotted in the village, which rather excited Sue Roberts and she told us with shining eyes how she had been stopped on the pavement outside her house and asked what she knew of the Fletchers.

'Nothin' to do with me, I sez. Dun know 'em at all. Quiet folk, with a couple of grown up kids, one of whom is not right in the 'ead after an accident. Didn't say no more. None of my business.'

She paused to control her indignation. 'Course, I sez, if I was one of their sort, the huntin' and ridin' lot, I'd a knowd a lot more. But as it is, Mrs Fletcher don't give me the time of day hardly. But I do feel sorry for the girl, that Melissa. Matea says she's really lovely, she is. Well, there you go.'

That phrase usually signalled the end of a discussion with Ms Roberts, as she would  then bustle off doing useful things around the house.

One day at the beginning of November, I met James. I watched from my study window as a young man strode towards the house. I then heard a door close and a male voice join with Matea's.

Shamelessly unable to restrain my curiosity, I crept out, crossed the stone-flagged hallway and peeked round the kitchen door quietly. I presumed that James had lost his shyness, as he and Matea were in each other's arms and embracing passionately. They sprang apart at my discreet cough, and Matea, blushing, introduced James to me. He too was red faced, but more I believe from anger than embarrassment.

'Hi,' he said with a slight open-palmed wave.

'Sorry...er, um. I've just come round to see Matea. Had an argument with Mum, and, er, needed to get out...'

'Will you stay and have some tea?' I invited, curious to know more about this likeable lad. 'Matea, pop the kettle on.'

She quickly did as bidden, and I took in what I could of my young neighbour while remaining, just, on the right side of good manners. He was tall and slim, and wore a short-sleeved teeshirt revealing fashionably tattooed arms. A long sleeveless jacket was matched with the tightest possible trousers. With his stubbly beard and his  side-cropped hair, he looked every inch the urban hipster. I gestured to them to be seated, and he and Matea placed themselves on opposite sides of the table and I sat on the third side.

'Well, James, good to meet you at last. I'm sorry about your father.' This had been my first chance to offer condolences.

'Yes, well. Thanks. I believe your husband is working on the case? Do you know how far they've got yet? Have they found the bastard who did it?'

'No, we don't discuss cases between us,' I lied. 'Not protocol.''

'Agh!' A little squawk from Matea and her anguished expression reminded us both of the girl's close experience of the horror of the sudden murder. He turned to her, all concerned.

'I'm sorry, Matty. I forgot you saw the guy. Didn't mean to bring it all up again. Here...'

At this he stood up and went over to her, putting his arm around her shoulder. At that point I thought it better to leave. But curiosity caused me to turn at the door, tea-mug in hand, and put this outrageously nosy question to him,

'By the way, if you don't mind my asking, what was your argument about? I thought you got on well with your mother.'

'I do,' he admitted, 'but not when she's bloody unfair. She won't give me any money to spend unless I can account for it. So how can I ever treat Matea or take her out? My father left me some money, but all tied up in a trust fund until I'm twenty-five. And mum, of course, is in charge of it until then. I can't even go out with my mates! And she won't let me get a job, so I have to ask for everything.'

I agreed that seemed a bit rough, but thinking back to those of my students who frittered their money on drink, drugs and clubbing, added, 'Maybe she has her reasons.'

I left the lovebirds together and  went to see how Terri was doing.

# Chapter 8

I HAD BEEN LIVING the rural idyll for a few weeks when I decided to pay for Matea to take driving lessons. Dozens of trips – well all right, a few – chauffeuring Tony and Terri to doctors or outpatients- or eye-clinics or dentists were eating into my precious research time. It was either paying in exchange for time or else losing patience with the in-laws. So, more beneficial all round simply to shell out. David took Matea out on practice drives and Terri and Tony coached her on the theory from the DVSA guidebook.

While she was out on one of her paid lessons, a visitor arrived, a young blond man of distinctly Slavic good looks. He announced himself Matea's friend, by name of Zivko.

'Come in, Zivko, while you wait for her. Coffee?'

'Sure, why not?'

'You know Matea from English classes, I gather?'

'Yes, I am in the class above her, advanced. She is intermediate. We meet during the coffee break and after class sometime. But Matea, she is very, oh what, playful! She pretends she does not want to speak with me, but I know she really does!'

His arrogance chilled me: this was rapist-speak. I could see why Matea considered him 'a horrible man'.

'What if you're wrong, and she really doesn't like you? Is that not possible? You would respect that, right?'

'Oh, lady, I am not wrong! Well, maybe, a little. At the moment. But she will like me, I know.'

'And you will respect her decision if she doesn't?'

'Of course! But it will not be so!'

His grin indicated the impossibility to him of any girl wanting to turn him down. Maybe he had a track record to justify this view of himself. Then he went serious, and leaned over the table, speaking more quietly,

'But there is one problem. It is very big.'

'Oh, yes?'

'Yes. She is Croatian. We have history, our two countries, Croatia and Serbia.'

'Oh come one! That was years ago. The war must have finished before you were born. You surely don't hold grudges that long!'

'No, it's not just the latest war. Our countries have been enemies for hundreds of years. It goes very deep, in the blood, you know. Like you and the Irish, or you and the

Germans, or the French.'

I was losing patience. This nonsense had to stop.

'That's ridiculous! We may have had our differences in the past, but we're all good friends now. You can't blame individuals, especially young people, for the faults and problems of previous generations.'

'Oh, lady. It is not so with us. I have a friend, Piotr, who is from Russia. He, one time, he wanted Matea for girlfriend – she is the most beautiful girl in the school – but when she told him she was from Croatia, he did not want her any more. Maybe for one night in bed, but not for girlfriend.'

'Did he? Have his one night with her?' My prurient curiosity is insatiable. Something for my next confession.

'No, she is virgin. You know, very virgin! Cold, not like English girls in clubs!'

'And you – do you want her for one night, or as a girlfriend?'

'Oh, lady, I cannot tell you! But I am prepared to be her friend, even though she is from Croatia. I will do this great thing as she is so pretty.'

Just then we heard her driving-school car pull up at the front door. I opened it to her and warned her that Zivko was in the kitchen.

'Oh, no! Please, Doctor Julia, tell him to go away. I will go upstairs. Please, I am very busy, tell him.'

I did as instructed. Zivko at first laughed, and then his face grew drawn and his eyes narrowed. He strode across the kitchen and hall floors with barely concealed rage At the door he turned,

'Tell her, I'll be back.'

# Chapter 9

AFTER ONE AFTERNOON spent delightfully in the Bodleian library, I reached home at about eight o'clock to find Terri in the kitchen in what passed for her as a high state of excitement.

'You'll never guess what dramas we had here this afternoon,' she said, eyes darkening..

'Go on, what happened?'

'Well, Matea! That's the trouble with being so pretty and everything!'.

'What about her?' I became suddenly anxious.

'Well, there was almost a fight outside. James was here, from next door. He's been coming around a few times recently, I've noticed.'

I knew that but had not mentioned it to her in case it had got back to Catherine, but Terri, being fairly bored indoors, was fully attentive to what was happening in the immediate area around the house.

'And?' Old people can be so annoying!

'And there was some foreign chap, Vimto, Zimto..

'Zivko.'

'Yes, or something like that. Serbian, Matea said. An old boyfriend. He had come to persuade her to return to him, apparently. Turned up at the side door. Then James, who had been in the kitchen, went out to him and there was almost a fight – certainly a shouting match. Fancy, men fighting over a girl! I thought that sort of thing only happened on the soaps on television. Anyway, James must have won, as the other young chap ran off, screaming blue murder – only I couldn't understand any of it.'

'What happened then?'

'Well, I went down to see Matea. I mean, really. We can't have that sort of thing going on. I sent James home and heard the story from Matea. She seemed pretty upset by it all and swore it wouldn't happen again.'

The next day I took my coffee break early to hear the whole story from Matea. She was quite calm about it by now and full of admiration for the way James had stuck up for her, only hoping that his mother had not heard anything. She did say though that Zivko had cursed both of them soundly at the end of the fracas.

His parting shot was that the Serbs should have destroyed Croatia entirely when they had the chance, and that her first suitor, the Russian from the language school, was quite justified in hating her. However, Matea, flushed with confidence in James as her champion, was convinced that she had heard the last from her Serbian erstwhile admirer. I hoped she was right, but felt a pang of unease.

One Thursday afternoon, not long after the contretemps between the two suitors, I called into the kitchen for a cup of tea and found Matea there in tears. I invited her to my study to tell me her troubles, as I did not want Terri walking in on the scene. We took our mugs and lay them on coasters on the large leather-topped desk. There Matea showed me a piece of grey lined writing-paper, which I took and read.

### DOBRA ZNAM TKO SI TI!
### ZNAM ŠTO JE TVOJ OTAC UČINIO

'What does this mean?' I asked. 'What is this?'

Between sobs she explained, 'I went to school today as usual. Piotr and Zivko there. They look at me badly, you know, hard look, but not say nothing, anything. But when I get home, now, I open my bag, the bag on my back of books and notes I take in school, and there is this paper. It is horrible!'

'Why? What does it say?'

'It say "I know who you are! I know what your father did!"'

An escalation of hostilities. This is becoming serious.

'Look, do you know what it means, about your father?'

'No, I know nothing!'

'This is bullying. Did you show this to Mrs Fletcher? Does she know about it?'

'Yes, she know, now she know, and she says that I must not pay attention to this. That it is probably nothing, just horrible words. But she say maybe I think of leaving, of going somewhere else.'

'Oh, that's a bit strong. I'm sure she's right about it

being just words, but look, if anything like this happens again, I think we should tell David. He can give these lads an official police warning – that would scare them!'

She seemed somewhat reassured, but still deeply troubled. I suggested she took the next day off and did something to take her mind off this note. Going shopping usually does it for me.

'No, thank you. It's better I work. I go now to see Mr Deane. He must go for little walk, the doctor say. I take him into the garden.'

The following day Matea returned to work and said that she had texted her father to find out what the note could mean. Later that day she read his reply and fell into immediate despair.

'He say he want me to come home, that maybe is not safe for me here in UK. But no! I cannot. I do not want to leave you and Melissa and everyone here. No!'

I made no further mention of it, hoping she would simply calm down and get over it. Her mind seemed made up. Whether James had a part of that she did not say, but I suspected he was more of an inducement to stay than I was.

\*\*\*

One Saturday, some ten days after the mysterious letters, the weather turned from chilly drizzle to unseasonably balmy warmth. As I was driving back from the weekly shopping trip to the market in Tewkesbury and the Aldi superstore, I realised that I had not taken exercise of any sort for several days and determine to make the most of the pleasant

Winter's day. I heard myself humming a merry Fred Astaire melody as I approached the drive. 'Putting on my top hat, M-m-m-m-m-m, dusting down my tails,' I chirped, thinking fondly of the times when Nana Ivy and I listened to swing music and watched glamorous black and white Rogers and Astair movies from the 1930s.

Nana Ivy, the grandmother who brought me up while my own mother was immersed in subsistence farming in a muddy hippy commune in North Wales. I loved and respected the older woman. Lacking a formal education, she was never the less wise and mentally active. It was her example that encouraged me in a lifelong love of learning and in seeking justice for other people and animals wherever it was lacking. I was musing on his by the time I was turning into the Deane's drive.

Matea and Melissa had been walking together from the Fletcher house and reached the end of their drive, only feet away from mine, so I stopped and we waved.

'Hi girls. Going somewhere nice?' I called.

'Only to the Countrywide Store. Mrs Fletcher want some medicine cream – salve? – for one of her horses.'

'Bwave..Heart! Horse!' Melissa stuttered with a radiant look of joy. It was easy to be fond of this sweet girl, forever trapped in a child's mind.

'May I go with you? I'd like the walk.' Half a mile each way along the village road in their company would be a pleasure. They both accepted with vigorous nods and broad smiles, so I drove up to the Deanes' and dumped my shopping in the kitchen. David was sitting at the table sharing a coffee with his mother and promised to put the items away before some of them thawed.

I left via the rarely used front door, placed almost directly off the road, but useful only to pedestrians as vehicles other than buses were not allowed to stop there or park. The two young women had barely reached it, owing to Melissa's awkward gait.

We crossed together over to the footpath on the opposite wider grass verge, facing oncoming traffic, and strolled along three abreast, making small talk, mainly about the passing landscape. We passed the Norman village church, dedicated to St John the Baptist, and remarked on its unusual wooden tower. I admired the patience and affection shown by Matea, and the smiling good nature of her young charge, clinging to her arm.

The road was straight and uninterrupted, with occasional traffic passing. The sound of a car slowing down behind us did not surprise me, but the next action of the driver certainly did.

The car, a small blue Renault, passed us and then suddenly crossed over the carriageway and mounted the verge and footpath, blocking it off just feet in front of us. We both instinctively held on tightly to Melissa, Matea folding her arms around her and I taking her hand. The driver's door flew open and a dark-haired youth got out, shouting at Matea in what I took to be one of the Balkan languages.

He made a grab for her and she had to let go of Melissa to resist, screaming and waving her arms to fend him off. I joined in, punching at him, yelling 'Leave her alone and go away!'

I clutched at Matea's clothing and pulled her and

Melissa backwards away from the angry young man. When he realised that Matea was not going with him willingly, he continued shouting at her and he walked back to his driver's seat. Then he slammed his door, revved hard, and powered off with heavy use of gears, leaving deep muddy tracks in the soft verge.

The three of us stood stock still for a moment, then Melissa began wailing in real distress and Matea, herself shaking and upset, turned to console the girl, hugging her and speaking to her soothingly. We turned back for home at once and made our way as quickly as we could, arriving at the Fletchers' home in far faster time than on the outward journey.

Catherine was in the kitchen, engaged in stirring the ingredients of a cake. She looked up appalled at the sight of us three women stumbling in, in varying degrees of distress. Once Melissa was in a familiar setting, she calmed down at once and was distracted by being given the job of cake mixing.

'What,' both Catherine and I needed to know, turning to Matea, 'was all that about?'

'Oh, my God.' Matea had learnt that ubiquitous cliché. 'Luka, the boy from my town, he has come to take me home!'

'What?' That was both of us in chorus.

'He say that my father tell him to come for me, now, at once, and go with him to my home. He say that he marry me and I am not to go out from the house, because of all the horrible things that is happening to me.'

'What nonsense!' snorted Catherine, reflecting my own sentiments.

I chimed in, 'You can't just go like that! You must stay to finish your course, and your contract to look after David's parents and Melissa. We need you, Matea. You can't just go, like that!'

'However,' added Catherine with unexpected flexibility, 'if you really want to go home, I won't stop you. Nor will you, eh, Julia?'

'Of course not, if that's what you want. But is it?'

'No, no, I don't want to, but maybe... Please, let me think about this. It is very sudden.'

That seemed reasonable, so we left her to retire to her own room and Catherine returned to overseeing Melissa's culinary adventure, over which she was smiling happily. I took my leave and returned to tell David and a fascinated Terri all about the recent event.

We agreed that, from the following Monday, when Matea next reported for duty, no-one was to be granted admittance to the house without the express permission of both Matea and me.

We saw no more of Luka, although heard later that he had called at the Fletchers several times, but had not been allowed over the threshold. The following week, however, brought more bad news.

# Chapter 10

ON THE THURSDAY, as it was Matea's day off and David had some paper work on which to catch up, he decided to stay home while I went to Oxford for the day. He took me to the bus terminal in the morning and returned to collect me in the evening as arranged, and told me the news as we drove home.

'Matea's had another note,' he told me gravely. 'Apparently it says "Die, bitch", or something like it. Anyway, she's pretty upset as you can imagine. She found it in her bag when she was unpacking it, and cracked up. Catherine brought her round to see me, or you, whoever was in, to help reassure her. But I couldn't say much. What is there to say? I told that if anything else happened like this, I would take it in to forensics to see if anything could be found on it. I really can't do it yet as

I couldn't justify the expense of a DNA test, and I dabbed it with some powder but can't see any fingerprints.'

'Wow,' I uttered lamely. 'It's the first death-threat. I suppose you have to take it seriously, in case something really does happen to her. But don't you think it's just that Serbian boy being horrible and bitter again?'

'Possibly. Anyway, she's talking about going home. Not for good – and certainly not to marry that Luka chap – but just to see her father and find out what's behind that "We know what your father did" bit. Anyway, I told her to sleep on it, and discuss it with you tomorrow.'

When we got home, and over a welcome glass of wine, David showed me the note through the transparent medium of a sandwich bag, acting here as an evidence bag.

It was a sort of cheap grey notepaper, similar to the previous note, with the words scrawled on it in capitals

UMRI KUJO!!!

'I'm going to have a word with that Serbian lad and tell him that you can't go round making threats like that in this country.' David said, sounding annoyed. 'Of course, if I can prove that he wrote it, I could charge him with something, harassment at least, and get a protection order raised for Matea. With Catherine being a JP, that should be quite easy.'

# Chapter 11

I AWOKE THE NEXT DAY with wintry sunshine streaming through the cracks in the curtains, beckoning me to enjoy the clear, sunny weather. So after a quick breakfast and medicine-round with the Deanes, I donned scruffy clothes, collected a bucket and filled it with soapy warm water and a sponge, and did something I had been putting off for weeks.

All the family cars were garaged in the row of former stables running along the side of the drive. I reversed the Deanes' ancient Rover, to my mind practically a classic car, remembering how to use the gear stick and clutch, until the dusty old vehicle was sitting on the driveway. I set to washing away the months of grime and cobwebs. It needed to be sold but I was ashamed to take it to a garage for valeting in the state it was in.

As I stretched my sponge-wielding arm over the roof, I heard the Star College minibus drawing away from the Fletchers' carrying Melissa to another day of confidence-building and skills development, and shortly afterwards Matea appeared, walking up the drive towards me.

'Good morning, Matea. Sleep well?'

'No, Miss Julia. I cannot sleep. I am all the time thinking...'

She said that while beating her head with her fist.

'I must know what it means, the paper. What is about my father? How do the people "Know me"? Of course the boys at English school know me, so what does that mean? Oh, Miss Julia, I am so afraid.'

'Oh, I'm sure there's no need', I sounded insincere even to myself.

'No, I have decided. I must go home. Only for a week, no more. I must speak to my father. But....'

'Yes? What's wrong with that? Sounds sensible, and I'm sure we can manage for no more than a week.'

'Only, I do not hear nothing, anything, from my father after that phone call last week. He does not answer my texts, or emails. I try to telephone again, but nothing. I have only the number of Luka's family, and I do not want to talk to them!'

'Well, if you need help with booking a flight, or are short of funds, you have only to ask. It would be good to get to the bottom of this, and set your mind at rest about these dreadful notes.'

I left it that Matea would see if she could get a flight that weekend, then finished the car-washing job, showered and changed, and took the old Rover off for a drive to give its battery a charge.

Returning from a round non-stop trip to Evesham, I worked for several productive hours at home on the books I had, taking notes on paper and making attempts at drafts on the computer screen.

Some of the Burney family members had much more written about them than others, or they had written extensively themselves, like Fanny with her lifelong journals, so it was mainly a matter of reading what was already written and selecting relevant facts, noting where I obtained them.

The lesser known members, Susannah, Sarah Harriet, James and Charles Jnr, not to mention Mrs Meeke, have less written about them, and required more searching and researching in literary and scholarly journals. One reference excitingly led to another, so that research was as much fun as a treasure hunt.

I had hurried back to the books after lunch, not wanting to lose the thread of what I was reading, and would have gone on until nightfall without moving from my reading chair, had Matea not come to my room. I assumed she had come to remind me about the regular cup of tea we shared mid-afternoon. But this time her knock had a more urgent tone.

'Come in, Matea. I am just coming. I'd forgotten all about tea. Why? Whatever's the matter?'

Her face was flushed with anxiety etched all over her features.

'Please, Miss Julia. Something very stupid! I have my ticket to fly tomorrow, it is ready, but I forgot I do not have my passport. Mr Konstantinou has it!'

'Oh, bother. That is a nuisance. What does he keep it for?'

'I don't know. He says it is his guarantee that we complete our contracts here and do not run away as soon as we arrive. He say the government ask him to keep them. But please! This is urgent! I need my passport, now! I have to have it for my boarding pass! I ring him on the telephone but there is no answer, only a message: "Mr Konstantinou is away from his desk, but your call is important to him".'

'OK, right. Let's go and find Mr Konstantinou and ask him to give you your passport. Do you know where he will be at this time?'

'I think he is at his office, in Cheltenham. At the big building.'

There is only one tower block in the town, the fifteen - storey Eagle Tower. So to that hideous example of 1960s architecture we had to drive, as quickly as possible to be sure of finding him at work towards five o'clock on a Friday afternoon. We had to risk the unhelpful telephone message referring to a temporary unavailability.

The Deanes' Rover was still outside on the driveway, unlike my car locked securely in one of the garages, so I grabbed the keys to the Rover and we both piled in. We threw our handbags onto the back seat, and sped off as quickly as the speed restrictions allowed.

Matea was obviously tense and agitated, so I suggested as we drove along that she should telephone Catherine to explain that she may be late getting back to deal with Melissa's return from Star College. It would, so I could hear, be the first time she had let Catherine know of her plans of a week's visit home.

I could tell from the tension in her employer's voice coming over clearly through Matea's mobile, that Catherine was not best pleased to be told at only the last minute. At least the apologising and explaining took up a good deal of the journey, so that Matea's impatience had just the drive between the racecourse and the town in which to develop.

We went the way I assumed would miss most of the traffic hold-ups, straight across into College Road, turning right after the hospital. I then took the right-hand lane positioning the car to turn right into Bath Road. But at the lights, Matea called out suddenly as she studied a car crossing in front of us going left,

'That's him! That's Mr Konstantinou!'

'Crikey! The cars behind will love this!' I waited until the traffic on my left had finished turning left, then I followed them, leaving the right turners no doubt fuming as they had lost their green light by the time I allowed them to move.

The car Matea had noticed, which I asked her to describe, was a beige Volvo five or six cars ahead of us along the Shurdington Road.

'Is this what you want to do?' I asked.

'Please, yes. Follow him and when we get to his house, we can ask him for my passport.'

She was on the verge of tears, so I just got on with following the Cypriot businessman's car. By the time we made Coopers Hill, where the famous cheese-rolling competition takes place, the Volvo was but four cars ahead. Shortly afterwards it turned off left, so we did too but we were held up by a tractor pulling out in front of us from a farm lane. As we slowed right down, Matea's agitation was palpable.

'Perhaps he does not have it at his house! Perhaps it is in his office and he will not go back for it!'

Matea then invoked the Mother of God, as did I.

The tractor eventually pulled into a yard on the left and we could speed up to a normal country lane pace.

'Don't let's worry about that yet,' I tried to reassure her, but feeling far from confident myself.

About half a mile further up the single-carriage winding lane we passed a farm entrance on our right and Matea yelled out 'There! At the farm!'

Bother. I had to drive another half mile before finding a turning space. We drove back towards the farm and turned slowly into the muddy entrance. There was the beige Volvo, as were several other vehicles, from smart cars to battered agricultural vehicles. Leading off the muddy yard were several large sheds, like small hangars, with the farm house itself tucked well back behind them, accessed by a narrow drive.

'You go, see where he is. Meanwhile I'll ring David and tell him where we are and why we're here. He'll expect me to be home at this time, and wonder what's going on. Off you go. Konstantinou will have to be in one of those sheds, or in the house. I'll wait here.'

# Chapter 12

SHE LEFT THE CAR and hesitantly negotiated the mud and cow pats as I concentrated on telephoning my husband. I saw her look through the window of the nearest of the sheds. She turned to me and shrugged, spreading her arms in a sign of disappointment. Then she trudged on further to another, peering through the nearest window. She looked back and shrugged again, and then moved to one even further away. I got through to David's answering service and gave him a brief update of where we were and hoped we would be home before long.

I watched Matea as she peered through the window of the distant shed, standing on tiptoe to see into it. Then she seemed to freeze, turned towards me, and scurried back to the car, running and sliding on the mud as she came. I told David I had to go.

'What's the matter?'

'Just go, please! Go! Go quickly!' she almost shouted as she exhaled heavily.

I did as she bid. She was shaking with shock or fear and unable to speak. Once we got back onto the country road, I asked for the reason.

'Wasn't he there, Mr Konstantinou?'

'Yes, but…'

Just as she was attempting an answer we were distracted by the same wretched tractor that had held us up before. I stood on the brake as it swung out in front of us from the yard which it had entered some moments earlier, this time towing a trailer. It crawled along, spraying liquid mud in its wake. This leisurely pace added to Matea's alarm, and she clutched the elbow rest of the door as if that could help the old Rover to go more quickly. She spoke again, gasping at breaths.

'He was there, but…horrible!'

I wanted her to go on, but she was too troubled to speak.

As it reached the lane from which it had emerged earlier, the tractor turned into it, steadily and quietly going about its business. I revved up, first looking in the mirror. I saw a large dark SUV, an old Land Rover Explorer catching up with us and getting close to my rear bumper. Too close. I felt a sudden chill of anxiety. This towering sturdy vehicle pulled out alongside us and, despite it being a narrow single track country road, drove parallel with us. 'Idiot!' I muttered.

Then, instead of speeding past or falling back, it closed in. *Clunk. Cher-bunkkk.* My side mirror was smashed, the maniac vehicle continuing to bump into the offside of mine.

I automatically tried braking, to let the idiot overtake, but that was not his intention. He pulled back as I slowed and rammed my car from the rear, pushing it along.

Matea was crossing herself, as was I mentally, while gripping the wheel with white-knuckle tightness.

But my steering was of no more use than the braking. The bigger, stronger 4x4 was shunting my car into the left hand verge of the road, and at speed. I watched in apparent slow motion as we approached the verge, with just beyond it, a ditch from which were growing mature trees. I desperately tried to steer away. No use.

The bonnet of my car suddenly lurched downwards, into the ditch. At a dangerous speed a large tree approached the near side.

Suddenly *chakkkrrunk!*. We hit the tree. The top part of the front near side of the sturdy Rover partially collapsed inwards, the windscreen shattering into a million tiny pieces.

The girl's scream was cut short by that terrible metallic crash. It was hard to tell which sound came in which order. My ribs felt crushed under the instant jolt of the safety belt's restraint and the stifling air bag instantly inflating, as glass and twigs flew into my face.

I punched a hole in the windscreen in front of me, shattering more glass fragments onto the bonnet as I wanted to see the vehicle which had done this to us. I could just make out a tiger's roaring face imprinted on the back of the dark vehicle speeding away in front of us, then all I was aware of was my breathing and of a warm dark syrup trickling into my eyes and down my face. At least those gasps told me I was still alive, and conscious. With the back of my hand I wiped away the glutinous blood from my eyes and wondered what the hell to do next.

When I could think more clearly, I looked over to Matea who was now sitting back, eyes closed, with the narrow branch of the tree touching her face. There was blood on that too, and her mouth was open. At least there was the sound of rasping breath, so I knew she was still alive. Thank God.

I fumbled for the belt fastening, unclicked it and groped down around the footwell for my mobile phone, thrown off my lap by the crash. Sitting up again I had to avoid the car roof at the top of the window, buckled downwards by the impact with the tree. I dodged my head around it and desperately jabbed the speed dial number for David. He answered, to my immense relief. I cut across his greeting,

'David. Emergency. There's been an accident. Call an ambulance, now, please. Straight away. Matea's been hurt and I can't drive. Come out for me, please!'

'Where the hell are you? You said something a minute ago about being at a farm near Sherdington.'

'No, it's past there, nearer Painswick. Hurry! It's a country road, on the left. There's a farm at the corner, red brick I think. Just after a row of cottages. We're down there.'

'Well, leave your phone switched on and I'll get it tracked if we can't find you. I'll ring the ambulance people right now. And the traffic police. And do you need the fire service to cut you out?'

I looked around. 'No, I don't think so. But hurry up. Matea's still unconscious.'

Just then the dreaded tractor loomed up, the same that had held us back earlier on. The driver braked surprisingly quickly to a stop and climbed down from his lofty cab. He reached into a trouser pocket for a mobile phone and began speaking with the emergency services almost immediately. At least he knew exactly where we were, and gave accurate directions. Then he bent down and peered through our now empty windscreen.

'Don't worry, ladies,' he said with a broad country accent and unwonted cheeriness. 'They'll be yar in a jiffy, and you'll be all right then. Just hold on until they comes. Nasty accident this. Lost control, did you?'

I did not know whether to bless him for his attention or curse him for blaming my driving. I said nothing.

'Have y' got a tow rope, Missus? I could fix it up to this tractor and have you out of here in no time, assuming yer front axle's OK.'

'That's really kind, but I belong to the AA, thanks. They'll sort that out. Right now all I'm concerned about is my friend here. She's still unconscious and I don't know how badly hurt she is.'

Just then Matea gave a reassuring groan and whimpered for a moment. Then asked something in Croatian.

'I'm sorry. You'll have to speak English. But just sit still, and wait for the ambulance people to come. Try not to move, or speak. David's on his way.'

She drifted into a sleepy state, whether conscious at all I could not tell. It may have been nature's way of deflecting the pain she must be feeling. The kindly farm-worker removed the tree branch poking through the window and got back on his phone to see where the ambulance was.

'It's on its way,' he declared. Not long afterwards, we

heard the reassuring siren and both an ambulance and marked police car arrived together.

By the time David arrived, I was wrapped in a silverised blanket and seated shivering in the ambulance, with Matea lying alongside, being checked over by a paramedic. The police had taped the area around the car and were taking careful notes and photographs of the scene.

David followed the ambulance as we were driven at speed, with siren wailing, to the trauma unit at the Gloucestershire Royal Hospital in Gloucester.

Once there I was examined by a pleasant young Polish woman doctor. She cleaned and taped up the cuts on my forehead with little strips of strong adhesive, and pronounced me healthy. However I was admitted  for an overnight stay in the hospital so that I could be checked again the following morning. Normal procedure for a head injury, apparently.

Matea was admitted as an in-patient and was taken off to a special care unit.

I barely slept, despite being given medication, reliving the awful moment when I realized the driver of the massive vehicle to the right of us intended doing us harm.

*Helpless – steer! – brake! – no use – the tree! – the ditch! – Oh no! – crash! – **kerchunk!** – death? – pain in my chest, stomach – breathe – blood....*

The next morning I underwent some tests and was declared sound. David called for me and took me home.

# Chapter 13

FOR MATEA, the situation was not so good. The Rover, despite its age, or maybe because of it, had not crumpled completely, but the passenger side certainly came off worse in the contest with the tree. My life was probably saved by the driver's air-bag, but on that age of vehicle there were no passenger side air-bags. Had we been in my own car, the side impact air-bag and curtain would have saved her from the head injuries she suffered.

An overworked but kindly senior nurse assured me that Matea's injuries were not considered critical. No lasting brain damage inflicted. 'Unlike poor Melissa', I muttered to myself. Just concussion and some memory loss that should well be restored in time. Cuts to her face and head were relatively superficial and cracked ribs would mend.

David and I heard this when we returned to the hospital in the afternoon  to visit her. We were relieved to see her sitting up, even though, with tubes inserted into her arm, her head bound in bandages and her eyes puffy and blackened, she looked worryingly damaged.

With some discomfort,  she managed a smile, 'Thank you to come to see me,' she said quietly, then paused to wince. 'Also the police have been. I have spoken to them but not remember very much. Only I see the tree, then nothing!'

We assured her that was fine and not to worry, nor try to do too much.

'Why I was in the car? Where was I going? You were there, too, yes? You drive the car. Your face?'

She looked with surprise at the adhesive strips on my forehead, presumably trying to work out why they should be there.

'Just relax and don't worry about anything. All you have to do is get better and come home..'

At that moment, we were joined at the bedside by James Fletcher wearing a concerned expression and clutching a plastic bag. He nodded in acknowledgement to David and me, and I stood back to let him draw closer to Matea's pillow.

'Hi, just brought you some things Mum said you might need in here. My God, you look awful!

He handed the bag over to me, with a slightly sheepish smile, and turned back to his beloved. I removed a hairbrush, toothbrush, pair of slippers and a nightdress, leaving a pair of panties discreetly in the bag. I placed everything in the locker beside the bed and made eye contact with David, flicking a look towards the door. He then suggested, with remarkable sensitivity, that we should not tire Matea, and that we would be back, either to collect her or visit her again the next day.

When we got to the door, I looked back to see James tenderly holding Matea's hand, his face close to hers.

David and I were cruising up the rural A38 between fields of horses and undulating ancient meadows, when my mobile rang.

'Hello? Nana Ivy?'

'How are you, Julia? I hear you've been in an accident. What happened?'

'I'm fine, thanks. It's a long story – tell you later. We're just on our way home from visiting Matea, who'd been my passenger, in hospital...'

'Well, stop right where you are,' she declared.

I signalled to David to pull over, and put the speaker volume up so that he could hear.

'Your mother is on the coach, right now, from London. She said she tried to phone you, but you weren't there. David's mother answered and told her you'd been in an accident. You'll have to go to Cheltenham bus station to meet her. She should be there at – let me see what I wrote down – four thirty five. Don't blame me for this! It was entirely her idea. Call me properly tonight if you can.'

David let out a pointedly loud sigh, and I swore his eyes were rolling. I breathed in deeply, taking in the consequences of this news and groping for ways to see it in a positive light. One mother in the house is bad enough – but two!

'It's four o'clock now. We'll just make it if we go right at Coombe Hill,' I suggested.

'By *The Swan*, I know. I've been on this road before. Your mother…,' he spoke with ill-concealed annoyance. 'How long will she be staying for, do you think? Where will she sleep? I don't suppose she's asked my mum and dad if they mind!'

I could not answer civilly, so chose not to say anything and we spent the rest of the journey in silence, until, while waiting for the London coach to arrive, I blurted,

'She's only doing it to be kind.'

But even I had my doubts, and mentally examined all the possible reasons for this sudden burst of maternalism. This was the mother, after all, who abdicated all responsibility for raising me. She recently gave me some story about one of the arrivals in her commune being something of a paedophile, and she thought it better to remove me from danger. But there were other things she could have done. Like leave the commune and get a job like an ordinary person.

The pain of a lifetime of feeling abandoned ran too deep for any show of affection from Helena now to equate with due compensation. On the other hand, my Nana Ivy had provided me with the best and most loving of homes. Remembering that, my feelings of hostility towards my crazy mother were modified by the time she emerged from the 444 coach from London.

I tried to think of pleasant things to say once we expended the usual trite enquiries during the drive home. Could not. In the end it was Helena who broke the silence.

'Your mother, Terri, sounds very nice, David. I'm

looking forward to meeting her.'

This was the mother who had avoided all occasions, including my wedding, when she could have socialized with my inlaws. Marriage was altogether too bourgeois. Now in her midfifties she had herself recently married. I snorted with laughter at the irony.

'You know that staying was her idea,' Helena continued breezily. 'I told her I didn't want to be a nuisance or make a fuss but she insisted there was plenty of room.'

David barely spoke, but I guessed from his expression he was finding it difficult to imagine his mother making wildly generous offers of hospitality.

'And how is the girl – Matea? Funny name, that. I suppose it's Matthew for a girl. Not too bad, I hope? Well, anyway, you won't be short of a helper around the house now, for a few weeks anyway.'

Few weeks! That was worse than I feared.

As we approached the house I bit my lip with anticipation of the meeting between Terri and my mother. Helena was no longer dressed like a superannuated hippy, but her clothes and shoes were, to say the least, well lived-in, and her hair a frizzy mess held back in a version of a pony tail by an elastic band. A newly acquired tattoo in the shape of a butterfly on her neck, and probably more elaborate ones unseen, did nothing to improve her looks.

Terri, whom I had warned in advance of our arrival, was waiting in the kitchen. Her eyes scanned my mother from hair to feet. Was that a shudder?

'Do come in, and welcome, er, Helena. So good to meet you after all this time.' She proffered her bony hand.

'Julia, dear, do see that your mother has a cup of tea. We could all do with one, I expect. How is Matea?'

She turned to David, who muttered about the patient doing well, and possibly coming home tomorrow, as the nurse mentioned.

David and I later showed Helena up to the first floor and to the guest room furthest from Terri and Tony's bedrooms. It still contained some empty tea-chests and unpacked cartons of linen from our London flat, so David quickly shifted them onto the landing while I made up the bed, inserting an electric blanket in case it had not been sufficiently aired. I brought in a fan fire to warm the room, but with most of Helena's adult life being spent in the damp and draughty farmhouse, she swore she was indifferent to the cold.

'How long will Helena be staying for?' asked Terri when I took up their supper on a tray. 'I said she was welcome, of course, …' I mentally supplied the ending of this sentence, and felt warm with embarrassment for my own flesh and blood.

'I have no idea,' I replied. 'For as long as she thinks she is needed, probably. With Matea laid up, and probably not fit to work for a few days, her ministrations will come in useful. You don't mind if she looks after the two of you during the day, do you?'

'Oh no, no. Not at all. But I would not want her to feel under any obligation to help us, you know. She has her own home now, I believe?'

I assured her that Helena would feel no such compunction, failing to mention that duty had never been a part of my mother's vocabulary up to now.

After our meal, David pointedly left us in the kitchen

and went into our sitting room 'to watch the football', whether or not there was any being screened.

In any case, Helena wanted to talk to me, and I to her.

'Well?' I opened the conversation as well as a bottle of white wine. 'What exactly brings you here? Don't say you were worried about me after my accident? That would be a first!'

'Now, don't be like that,' she said, looking hurt. 'I do care about you. I've missed you like mad since you left London, even if we weren't always in and out of each other's flats. It was a comfort to me to know you were there, just a floor above.'

'What about Ronald? You've only been married, what? Six months? Don't say you've left him already!'

'No, nothing like that. When I heard about the accident, and from Mrs Deane, not from you – I never would have heard a word from you – we talked it over and Ronald – he's such a dear – he said that he'd go to stay with his sister in Bournemouth while I was gone. She was fine about it. No, marriage is really suiting me. Haven't you noticed how well I look?'

She did look healthy, apart from having put on some weight. 'From not smoking,' she explained to my amazement. At one time she would have lit up any dried leaf or resin and inhaled it rapturously.

'For one thing,' she went on, lowering her voice, 'Ronald has taught me what love means.'

'Oh, puh-lease! What do you know about love? One minute you're shagging everyone you fancy, and now you go all Mills and Booney! For God's sake, I think I prefer you the way you were. At least there was some honesty about your love life, not sentiment. I thought you were all about authenticity!'

'Oh, you are hard. I don't know where you got that nasty streak in you from. Not from my side, I'm sure of that.'

Seeing that she knew little about my father, other than he was the alpha male of the commune and dominated it for years like a cult-leader, I'm not surprised she knew little of his genetic make-up.

# Chapter 14

'YOU DON'T WANT to hear me, do you! Ronald has taught me what love really means.' She went serious and leaned forward to emphasise the profundity of her remarks, 'It means thinking of the other person, of being considerate, putting yourself out. That's what Ronald does. He's shown me that that's what it is, really, in actions, in how he lives. I feel that by being with him and trying to be more like him I'm a different person now, changed. Now don't look at me like that!'

My cynicism had reached nausea-point.

'In any case, 'she went on, undaunted. 'I feel I've gained some faith. Not religion, not like you. I could never accept all that Catholic – I won't call it mumbo-jumbo – but all those rules and words you use. I'll never understand how a clever girl like you could fall for all that. But, now, stop, let me finish. Ronald doesn't go to church, but he believes, and I understand that. He believes in something, some life-force, something that causes everything to exist and come together.'

'Not now, Helena. I can't take all that right now. We'll

have a good chat some other time.'

But she went on regardless.

'There is something, call it God if you will, that brings things together, like all the atoms and molecules, and that causes everything to be. It's what Ronald says. In a way it's force of love, of attraction, that causes things to come together, and not stay apart.'

I must have frowned. She took it as my doubting what she said, not that I couldn't bear to hear this clap-trap.

'Don't you see, this thing we call love – sounds like a song, doesn't it? – well, this attraction, it doesn't just bring everything together, that would lead just to a gigantic big mass, but it is what brings them to life as well. So love, this power or force of love gives life, well, to living things, but that's all on account of this force.'

'Let the Force be with you!'

'Oh, I knew it. I'm trying here to make sense of something important, and you just trivialise it! I'm trying to be serious, and don't have your gift for language, so hold on while I try to explain.'

I struggled through an overpowering urge to go to bed and fall into the first deep sleep of ages. I heard her voice drone on; 'What I'm saying is that there is something, out there yes, but in everything too, in such a way that things exist and life exists, and so what is behind it all is some great Cause and Sustainer of life and of everything.' She made quotation marks with her fingers around those key words. 'Otherwise, ' she went on, 'things, atoms, molecules, would just whirl around, all individually, and nothing would ever come together and be joined into things. So, basically, love is the basis, the whole point, and we human beings can somehow join in with this by loving.'

Her eyes were gleaming. She was enthused. I imagined she had thoughts like these in her hippy days. I began to make connections with my own faith, but she misread my expression.

'Stop looking so – so, like you don't follow me. When I say love I doesn't just mean sex, though that really does involve coming together, but in every way that helps and not harms other living beings. Do you get me?'

'I get the point about being loving to everything. Haven't I always said that? That's why I'm vegetarian. You always scoffed at that. You could even have the animals on your farm slaughtered and eaten, creatures you had known!'

'Oh, you're just being difficult!'

'Well, why can't you accept that this Force of Love, as you call it, this cause behind everything, is the God that I believe in? After all, St John says "God is love".'

'Huh, you could have fooled me! Your God seems so full of rules, all "Thou shalt not" and "You can take Communion here, but not there", and all of that. My Force is big.' She stretched her arms out wide. 'You don't half make your God small. You talk about him as though he were a man!'

'You mean Jesus?'

'No, I mean you say "God does this and that, says this and that, likes and dislikes, wants and hates" and so on. I don't see how this Force can be like that.' She paused, looking thoughtful. I had never heard her like this before, taking anything so seriously. I let her carry on, ' Ronald can explain all this so much better. Oh dear. What I mean is, you ask your God for things like you would a person, a king or something, to intervene, to answer prayers and such like, as if he can hear you, even when you're not speaking out loud. But you can't expect this Force to be like that. It's above all that.'

'Doesn't care, you mean?'

'No, of course a force cannot care. Not for individuals, any more than for cells or pieces of things. But the force itself, it's a power, like electricity. You can't see it, but it's there. It is what drives everything, brings everything together. That's what it is. It's – a law of nature, of physics.'

'But things die in nature,' I was floundering. This all seemed too vague, too New Ageish.

'Yes, but in nature nothing really dies.'

'What?'

'No, it simply changes from one form to another. Ronald says it's a fact of physics. When we die, our bodies change eventually into bits, carbon and things, that feed new growth, new life. Plants grow out of bodies, worms feed, soil is made. That is what I mean. There is this force that brings about and sustains life, but is not interested in whether individual lives are happy or not. A force cannot be "interested" or have feelings. It just is. That's how it is.'

My head was spinning. I was too tired for this. There had to be a flaw in it, but I was not up to working it out. I struck out instead with what thoughts just popped into my head.

'But if this force is the togetherness of things, a loving power bringing all things in being, don't you feel that people need to get together themselves to worship this force – only we call it God?'

'No, not at all. Come together by all means, all the time. That follows this law of nature. But not to worship it, not do things to "appease" it as if it would stop being a force of love if you didn't do or say all the right things. You think it all depends on you! As if we people, coming together to sing hymns and say prayers and do a lot of ritual stuff, can have any influence on this force which is not a person at all!'

My eyes were glazing over despite my best efforts.

'Oh come on, girl! This is simple. You don't need any of that "I believe in" stuff. Just be loving and that's the secret.'

I stirred myself. This is my mother, my bloody mother, telling me my whole belief system is nonsense and unnecessary. How dare she? This was Ronald talking. She would never have dreamt up all that by herself. Then I had a thought, a clincher.

'Ah, but Jesus, though. That was his message, through and through. Love was the whole point of it. We had to be loving just as his father, God, is loving. You want to keep the loving and drop the God-part. It doesn't work like that!'

'Well, yes, he was a good man, I grant you. Showed how far love should go – died for it, even. But all that "Saviour" business. What's he saved me from? I don't believe in heaven and hell, so how can I be saved from hell?'

This was too deep for me at this hour, not long out of hospital. I felt a sudden urge to droop, to fall asleep and put this wretched argument behind me. I bade her good night and went to bed. But sleep eluded me. Bloody mother!

# Chapter 15

AFTER THAT DISTURBING discussion, I avoided my mother whenever I could. I could not bear the thought of a resumption of that discourse. Sometimes I found myself considering her argument, and could see how it made some kind of sense for her. I had neither the time nor energy to go there. It had been an effort for me to become a Catholic, ten or so years ago, which I did because of marrying David. And it had brought me a peace of mind, the dependency on a reliable Father-figure I had lacked in my childhood. Regular Mass-attendance had provided a rhythm to the week. Prayer helped take me out of myself to think of others. No, I was not going to let that awful woman cause more trouble in my life.

Actually, in the absence of Matea, Helena was making herself useful around the house. To a point, although she was generally too wrapped up in herself to notice when Terri or Tony needed something, and her constant chatter wore them down. Terri suggested she spent more time with me. Oh no. It then occurred to me to wonder whether Catherine could make use of her in looking after Melissa for a few days. Brilliant!

We walked together, my mother and I, down the two drives, the first over tarmac and brick, the next over shingle. Catherine, through her kitchen window, waved us to the gun-room door.

'Oh do come in,' bid Catherine while shushing her dogs and pulling them back from jumping up at Helena. 'You must be Julia's mother? Helena, isn't it? I've been so longing to meet you. Do go through.'

Helena was smiling as she looked around the untidy kitchen, with dogs sniffing and wagging their greetings, and muddy foot and dog prints decorating the floor. This was her kind of place. More upmarket than she had been used to, but definitely her style.

Catherine took to her, too, and seemed delighted that Helena would be willing and able to spend time with Melissa when the latter was not at college.

So Helena took to passing her days between the Fletchers and the elder Deanes. In the evenings, she seemed to shadow us, either in the kitchen or the sitting room. The only place David and I could talk privately was in bed. Talking and sleeping were all we were doing there these days.

David was not assigned to our vehicle case, although he had it upgraded from a traffic accident to a case of possible manslaughter. The deliberate act of forcing us off the road was taken seriously, particularly in the light of the still unsolved Fletcher murder case.

I asked him about it one night as we were lying both staring at the ceiling while the television in Helena's room was blaring on full volume just above our heads. Raucous canned laughter gave way after a while to the background music to an old black and white film. Fortunately Tony and Terri, on the other side of the house, are both sound sleepers and are not kept awake. Unlike us. I first asked about the murder enquiry.

'How is the enquiry going? You've not mentioned the Fletcher murder for a while now. It's stuck, yeah?'

''Fraid so. We've got some leads, but nothing much. We've been busy with other cases since that, don't forget our unit covers the whole of the three counties. That Ian Fletcher led such a complex working life he could have had a score of enemies, and we're patiently working through them – everyone from retired IRA Provos to Libyan gun-runners and agents of his he left in the lurch. Not easy asking these chaps if they'd mind terribly helping police with their enquiries. I've got one lot of MI5 investigators working round the clock and another lot trying to obstruct me at every turn. It's a nightmare – but we'll get there.'

'And our case? Any further forward on who tried to kill us?'

'Yes, some. That big black SUV had been picked up on some of the ANPR cameras, but then lost in country lanes somewhere near Gloucester. The number plates were false. Probably taken from a scrap yard years before, so no lead to its provenance. The distinctive tiger print on the spare wheel cover at the back should make it easy to trace, once it surfaces again. But my bet is that it won't be used for a while, and with new number plates.'

'What about the farm buildings where Matea had that fright? We still don't know what caused her to dash back to the car. Has she said any more, other than what she told me at the time, that Mr Konstantinou was there, but for some reason she didn't feel like asking him for her passport? Just came running as if she'd seen a ghost.'

'No, she's not said anything. Absolute blackout, apparently. I put a squad out there first thing the next day. All they found were sheds filled with sheep! Of course, if something had been going on, any trace was buried under sheep droppings. There were loads of tyre tracks in the mud from different vehicles, but nothing that could be distinguished. I've been trying to get a warrant to search Konstantinou's premises, but with little to convince a JP, other than a "something" that caused a young woman's real or imaginary fright.'

'You could get a warrant signed by Catherine,' I pointed out.

'Hardly. She's too close. Wouldn't look good. It's not like scaring off a bolshy teenager from harassing Matea. This Konstantinou bloke would have his lawyers up in arms if we didn't go strictly by the book. Don't worry, I've got people keeping an eye on him. And if there's anything to connect him with that SUV, we'll have him.'

# Chapter 16

THE GREAT DAY came when James called round with the news that Matea was home. He had collected her from the hospital that morning and she was resting in her room. I grabbed a jacket and walked with him to Catherine's kitchen, where he made a pot of tea and took up a mug to the convalescent. His mother poured ours, and I asked her how Melissa had taken to Helena.

'Oh, wonderfully well. They're best of friends. It's so good of you to spare her like that. Mel will be delighted, of course, when she comes home from college today, to find Matea's back, although looking at her I can't imagine she'll be much use for a bit yet. So if Helena would carry on…'

'Of course. She'd love to.' I felt confident of that.

'After the accident, when Matea didn't come home,

poor darling Mel  was deeply upset, of course, but James is the one who went all sloppy. He almost gave up eating, studying, everything. I don't know. Anyhow, I've offered to let him throw a party for her, a sort of "welcome back", "glad you are better" kind of thing. Also it'll will do for an early Christmas party. Just for a few of his friends from the  course at Worcester. Plenty of booze and bits to eat and loud music, that kind of thing. Next Saturday evening. I was going to send him round to apologise in advance for the noise and so forth. Hope it won't keep you awake. There won't be too much traffic – they're coming in just a couple of cars, all piled in together. Mostly boys, with just a few of the girls from their class. Well, apparently James's set don't really know many other girls – not socially. That's maths students for you! Sensible of them. All very hardworking, apparently. Just James's closest friends. Matea should be in her element with all that attention. Well, I would have been at her age, I can tell you!'

'Oh, good. That sounds cool. No, of course we don't mind, it's a great idea. Nice for her. Although I don't get the impression she's crazy about lots of male attention. Rather shy when it comes to men, I thought.'

'God yes. She's like a nun! I think that's why all these bloody youths keep chasing her – Little Miss Hard-to-get. Of course, that's the way to trap a chap into marriage, we all know that!'

She went thoughtful. 'Just wish that James wasn't so smitten. But there you are – you can't put an old head, etc. You know.'

James appeared and was happy to take me up to visit Matea in her bedroom. She was sitting up in her bed, with her head still bandaged. She was looking pale but managed a smile and I took her hand, assuring her that we could cope until she was well enough to resume her duties.

The next day she was on her feet and taking brief walks in the chilly early December air in the Fletchers' garden.

\*\*\*

On the Friday, the week after our crash, she called in on me. I stopped work willingly and sat her on one of our comfortable armchairs in the sitting room. She was looking and sounding stronger, with some colour in her cheeks. The darkness and puffiness around her eyes had gone and her natural good looks had returned.

'Oh, I am so happy,' she beamed. 'Tomorrow there will be a party, a small party – for me! I will meet some of James's friends and Mrs Fletcher, she is making for us a special drink – a "push"..'

'I think you mean "punch" – but that's great!'

'Yes, to say the truth, I was thinking Mrs Fletcher was not liking that James and I are ...an item. Yes? When I was in the hospital James told me that he loved me!'

I had never seen her look so happy.

'Oh, great. Good for you. That's lovely. How many people are coming?'

'Oh, I think only small number, no more than ten. They are close friends of James.'

'And Melissa?'

'Oh, no. Melissa – it will be too much for Melissa. She will sleep in another room, the most far from the sitting room, so that she can sleep. But, I have a question. What will I wear? What you think?'

'Oh heavens, I wouldn't think of dressing up. Too informal. Your new jeans and that red blouse of yours would be fine. I'm sure none of the boys will dress smartly. It'll all be jeans and tee-shirts'

She went off with a couple of bottles of Prosecco that we had around, agreeing that Mrs Fletcher may like them for her punch.

The next day was cold, with lowering cloud and a heavy sort of dampness in the air that I never noticed in London. The last of the leaves had fallen and were lying in moist heaps where David was raking them. I did the usual Saturday morning shopping and put in a couple of hours with my books before lunch.

In the afternoon I left my reading to join David in gardening chores and we passed several happy hours in unaccustomed physical labour, filling wheelbarrows and dumping leaves and tree debris into wooden compost stalls in the further reaches of the garden.

There was something pleasant in the aches and tiredness, and the feeling that we deserved a large gin and tonic before the evening meal that Helena made for us. We all sat down together afterwards to watch a Scandinavian detective programme on BBC4 and then went wearily to bed. The beat of an overamplified bass in recorded music drifted over from the Fletchers, but did not keep us awake. As Londoners we were used to hearing all manner of noises, from screaming sirens and rowdy drunks, to the thump of heavy-metal music from neighbouring flats and even from some passing cars.

The next morning I did not consider collecting Matea for Mass as we used to do. Hangovers and early morning services hardly go together. David drove Terri and me and after the liturgy we shared a coffee and biscuit with the priest and other congregants, many of whom asked after Matea, commiserating with expressions of sympathy and offers of help, should we need it. The three of us spent the short journey home dissecting the Advent homily and passing judgement on the choice of hymns.

At the entrance of the drive we were flagged down by James who came running down his towards us.

'Have you seen Matea?' he asked, panting, his eyes darting round the interior of the car as if she had stowed away in it.

'No. Why? Not since Friday. But you had your party last night!'

'Yes, but she left during it, and hasn't come back, and she's not answering her phone. It's switched off. I thought she might be with you. Y'know, at church?'

'Not with us,' David answered. 'But she might be with Tony. He doesn't come with us, and she may have popped up to see how he is. Have you knocked?'

'I did, but no-one came.'

We drove up the house and waited for James to join us. He then accompanied us inside. We stood in the hallway and called out 'Matea?' but there was no response from upstairs. Helena appeared from the kitchen, wiping her hands from chopping onions as I could tell from the pungent aroma.

'No, love. She's not been here. Not seen her at all. Tony's been sleeping since you left, and I must have been round the back, earlier, with the bins, when you called.'

Helena accompanied Terri upstairs while David, James and I did a thorough job of scouring through each of the downstairs rooms, looking under tables and behind sofas, in case Matea had succumbed to the drink of the night before and was still snoring.

But nothing. I made a herbal tea for Tony and filled a filter jug of coffee for the rest of us, then took a tray of hot drinks upstairs while David and James went out to look through the garages, old stables and the barn.

After a while the two men returned and, as he had promised to James, David put a call through to his police colleagues informing them of a 'missper' and asking them to report any sightings of a slim young Croatian woman, about five feet eight or nine, dark brown eyes, with a partly shaven and bandaged head. He asked James to describe what she had been wearing, and repeated the description of a red blouse and tight denim jeans, black ankle boots with stiletto heels. And probably a thick navy jacket.

'Yes, I know,' David said to the voice on the other end, 'It's not long – and yes, the woman's over eighteen. But,' he insisted, 'this is a case of a young foreign woman. She doesn't know many people round here, yet alone in the UK. Listen, some of the ones she does know have been sending her threatening letters. So, kindly take this as serious. Also she was involved in a traffic incident recently where she and my wife were run off the road and we haven't caught who did it yet. The girl was hospitalised and is still in recovery. So you see, it really does warrant urgent action.'

While still talking, David had walked through to the

kitchen, and indicated James should precede him. I poured coffee for the three of us and we sat around the table to discuss this event further.

David finished his call but, just before we began discussing the situation, Catherine appeared, so another mug was assembled.

'Sorry. Saw your side door open. Any luck?'

'None so far,' James replied disconsolately.

'I'm sure there's no cause to worry, despite what I said to the police,' said David in his most assuring voice. 'After all, one thousand people went missing every single day in this country, the UK, last year. And they're just the ones reported to to the police. Three quarters of them were located and problems resolved within twenty-four hours. So there's still loads of time. Really, there's no need to worry.'

I was not convinced.

# Chapter 17

IT WAS SO OUT of character for Matea to go off like that. At the least, she would have called here, if she just wanted to get away. I smiled wanly, trying to hide my real concern.

'What happened?' we both asked at once. James and his mother looked at each other, then James answered.

'Well, I don't know. I got really smashed and don't, like, remember anything. All I know is that I woke up with, like, a crashing head, and she wasn't there. Oh God!'

He nearly burst out crying, but held himself back with effort.

'Well, I can fill in some gaps there,' offered Catherine. 'There was rather a lot consumed last night. All my punch went, and lots more besides. Wine and spirits. And they'd been drinking before they came. Some of James' friends are still sleeping it off! Snoring their heads off in my sitting room!

Anyway, I was still awake, around midnight I think, and in my bedroom at the time I heard James and Matea having the most awful slanging match. I never heard anything like it from either of you. She was really upset with you, James. I don't know what you must have done to get her so wound up.'

'Nothing! I don't remember anything! I can't think of what we could have been arguing about. She seemed so happy, as I remember. We started fooling around with iPads, looking at funny YouTubes and stuff, but from the time we started drinking, I must confess I can't remember anything at all. I don't know if any of my mates do. I'll have to go and ask them.'

'Hold on. What happened then?'

Catherine picked up the thread.

'As I said, you two were really at daggers drawn. That was about a couple of hours after the party started. Some time, as I say, around midnight. I don't know what the others were doing, but with all that music blaring, they probably couldn't hear a word anyway! You went outside for your spat, and I was just above you, that's how I heard you rowing. But what it was about I couldn't tell. It didn't last long, and you both went back inside. I looked in on Melissa not long after, in case you'd wakened her up. She hates it when people shout at each other. That's when I heard the front door bang. I thought I could hear a car engine too, but cannot be sure of that. The music was quite deafening.

Some time later, I went down and found you all

sprawled over the furniture, or on the  floor. Sound asleep, all of you.  With the music still pounding. How do you do that?'

'On a loop.  Oh mother!'

'Anyway,  I turned it off, blew out the candles before they burnt the house down, and left you all to it. Honestly, you were so out of it, you couldn't even get to your own bed. It hasn't been slept in.

At least Melissa seemed oblivious, thank goodness. But she woke up asking for Matea. I had to confess I hadn't seen her. I didn't remember seeing her last thing, but then it was dark and there were bodies slumped all over the place, I didn't look too closely. I didn't know who was who.'

'Well, that seems fairly straightforward,' David suggested. 'You had a row – let me know when you remember what it was about, it could help us find her – and she upped and left. Maybe someone was waiting for her, someone she called, maybe. A taxi? Or maybe she was walking furiously away and someone picked her up. Let's hope it was someone she knew or thought they could help her. She may be happily asleep in some Good Samaritan's family home and will turn up full of apologies for having caused you a fright. Let's hope so, heh?

Meanwhile, you go back and see if the others are awake yet. And I'll come over in a bit to interview them. See if they can shed any light on it. While you're doing that, I'll drive around, just in case she is making her way back on foot having slept it off in a farm shed or barn somewhere nearby. You never know, so off you go and don't worry unless you need to. And it's far too early for that yet.'

'Well, what d'you reckon?' I asked David as soon as the Fletchers had left.

'Mmmm. Don't know. Looks pretty bleak, if you ask me. We ought to go looking for her in the first instance. She might not have got far, especially if she'd drunk as much as the lads had, and so shortly after leaving hospital. She might have slept under a hedge somewhere and now isn't sure of the way home.

Then there are some things I'll have to call in about. We may get a reading from her mobile, if she took it with her, and if she didn't, we could read her call history. Also there could well be witnesses who saw her along the road.'

'Unless she got into a car,' I ventured.

'True. She may have called someone to pick her up. I'll see if there are any cameras around that might show something.'

'On these country roads?'

'Oh, you'll be surprised. There are surveillance cameras all over, Automatic Numberplate Recognition cameras, those ANPRs, even in some villages. But I agree, it's hardly London and there could be miles of these country roads without anything. But it's worth finding out.

'When I get back, I'll go and see if any of her clothes have gone. Perhaps you could help there? I suspect you would notice more of what she wore than Catherine would. Also her passport. That could raise all sorts of questions.

'I wonder if Catherine could hear her going to her room after the row? Shame James can't remember it, but I know what it's like to be legless with drink – well, I remember from those far-distant days of my youth!'

'The others are likely to be as useless as James was if they were just as blotto.'

'True. Oh, I'd better warn them not to even think about driving today. The alcohol will still be rushing around their veins.' He paused to think for a moment.

Then sparked into action.

'Anyway I'll just pop upstairs and tell the Oldies that we'll be out for a bit and that lunch will be later than usual today. OK?'

David was always good at organising crises. Clearing up loose strands. Goes with his neat appearance and need to tidy everything into straight lines. Drives me crazy sometimes, but not now. Now I appreciate his taking charge.

He turned to go, but I suddenly chilled at a thought and blurted out,

'What if Matea was abducted – by Ian's killer? What if he had come back to finish the job, get rid of a witness, and Matea had walked right out into him? Oh God…!'

'Enough of that! We can't know anything of the kind, so don't go imagining things. And for goodness sake, don't voice those thoughts to Mum and Dad.'

Subdued, I agreed. Needless worries served no purpose.

He softened his tone and went into practical mode,

'Why don't you drive over towards Stoke Orchard? I'll go towards Tewkesbury. Can you take in Buzzards Lane? I'll do both directions of the A38 – for a few miles anyway. Don't go further than Bishop's Cleeve, and I'll not go past the roundabout outside Tewkesbury. If she is walking, she could well be within a couple of miles in either direction of here. Right? Let's go!'

We both left. I could hear him taking the back stairs to

his parents' quarters two at a time. I hurried to my car to trawl the country roads seeking the missing young woman.

I drove as far as the Court Farm shop beyond Stoke Orchard, calling in to see if Matea had been seen by anyone here. No luck, but the pleasant young assistants promised to look out for her and phone me if she showed up. I gave my number to the young woman who tapped it into her smartphone. She and the youth, who was carrying trays of vegetables inside, remembered her from the times she had made the shop the target of a lengthy walk, picking up some eggs, bread or vegetables to justify the trek. Her accent, friendliness and good looks had made her quite memorable.

By the time I returned home and walked over to the Fletchers, there were several young people, bleary-eyed and dishevelled, wandering around the driveway and garden.

They were accompanied by three boisterous, furiously wagging dogs, excited by the presence of strangers. The spaniel particularly was careening around, bumping into the Labradors and the young people's legs; having fun. His liveliness contrasted sharply with the humans' lugubriousness.

Apparently these hung-over specimens of the human race had been assiduously, if lethargically, searching behind bushes, into outbuildings and even as far as the lane at the back, and the stables in the field beyond; but found no sign of Matea.

I walked into the Fletchers' house as they circled aimlessly outside. At Catherine's invitation, I made my way to the spacious sitting room and sank into one of the deep sofas as she organised coffee. She shooed out the dogs, all of which had taken advantage of the chance to enter the forbidden room, with the spaniel having enjoyed bouncing onto each of the chairs and sofas in turn. Then she left me to see to Melissa, who was being shielded from the news that would only distress her.

One by one the companions of the previous night entered and draped themselves in chairs and sofas or perched on their arms. The two girls present, Alice and Krystal, looked particularly haggard, their make-up smudged and blotchy. The boys, introducing themselves as Hugo, Charles, Freddie and Thomas, looked as though they could resume sleep at any moment. A couple of other young men and the girlfriend of one of them, clinging to her man as though he was keeping her upright, stayed outside, wandering around with an air of dejection. James slumped on the floor in a corner, too distraught to join his friends on the furniture.

We sat around in glum silence, freezing slightly in the early December air as Catherine had opened several windows to ventilate the room. She had obviously tidied and vacuumed it thoroughly as there were no signs that the room had recently doubled as a dormitory for drunkards.

David arrived and, performing just like a detective from an Agatha Christie novel set in a stately home, solemnly asked questions of the group. There was much furrowing of brows as each tried hard to recall events.

They remembered meeting James and Matea at Theoc House, the trendy café bar in Tewkesbury, for tapas and burgers. They had then moved on in convey to James' house for drinks and a stay-over. All had the impression that Matea was happy, even bubbly. The girls expounded on how she had been. They obviously considered her to be their friend, despite not being a fellow student. They described how she and James had become a real 'item', with their arms around each other when they walked or sat together. How they had eyes only for each other.

James was, in my opinion, by far the most attractive and self-assured of his group, and I wondered if the others had felt somewhat outclassed by him in many ways, and if there was any resentment or envy there. Maybe even jealousy of his having 'paired off' with such a catch as Matea. Could that be a sufficient motive to …? But I did not want to think about that, the worst that could happen. They were all on the same maths and business courses, and seemed decent, rather shy, even conventional, young people, despite some alarmingly spiky haircuts and facial piercings on some of them.

'Did Matea say anything, anything at all, that you remember, out of the ordinary, or of possible significance?'

'Only the big announcement. That she and James were going to get married and move to the States,' said a bespectacled lad with rather lank straight hair falling onto his shoulder.

James chewed his lip anxiously and glanced quickly at the door. He blurted, 'That's not common knowledge yet. I don't want it getting round. Anyway, there's a lot to do before we can go – work permits, green-cards and all that. Matea's got an uncle in Denver who could get me a job in his company, but it's not settled yet. I don't want Melissa knowing. She'd be too upset.' I wondered if Melissa was the only person he did not want to find this out.

The one who had mentioned the news shuffled with embarrassment. So David took control.

'I'm sorry, James. But that's just the sort of thing we need to know. Anything else, big or small?' He wanted to prompt them further. 'When do you intend to go? And is it your idea or hers?'

'It's both of ours. I really love her and want to marry her. But she wants to go now, and I want to finish my course. I'm in my final year and want to get it done. But Matea is really spooked by those notes she got – that Serb bastard! She has written to her uncle to see if she can stay with him until I join her.'

'Right,' said David. 'So could that have been what you were arguing about? That she wanted you to go straight away and you didn't?'

'Possibly,' uttered James in the most forlorn voice. 'But I can't remember!'

I felt a surge of pity and affection for the young man. Who hasn't crossed swords with someone and found the consequences far more serious than they had imagined?

Then my thoughts turned inwards. How could she do that, or even think it? How could Matea, my young friend – or so I thought – want to leave just like that? How could she have been prepared to abandon me with my elderly charges, and Melissa with her huge emotional dependency? I found my stomach knotting with indignation. It was a betrayal. A hurtful betrayal that Matea had not thought me trustworthy enough to confide in me. Maybe she thought I'd leak it all to Catherine, and cause trouble prematurely. But really, just to take off, without a word to me. How could she? After a few deep breaths I told myself to remember what Nana Ivy would say, quoting Madame de Staël, 'To know all is to forgive all.'

So I would have to wait to know more.

# Chapter 18

.

AS DAVID AND I went upstairs to Matea's room, shown the way by Catherine, he drew out latex gloves from his pocket, gave me a pair and put another on himself. I stretched the gripping fabric over my fingers and palms. He then gave me a plastic bag. 'For evidence', he whispered.

I asked just as quietly if he could notify all ports and airports.

'Hardly!' he replied. 'If a grown woman wants to take herself off, we can't do anything about it. It's not as if she'd be going to Syria! She may even be going back to Croatia to tell her Dad first. Look, I'll find out from that uncle in Denver if she shows up there. Meanwhile, just help me look for something, anything, that might help us know where she's gone.'

.

Catherine stood watching us at the doorway as we looked around the room. The bed was made up neatly, obviously unslept in. I casually drew a black embroidered cardigan off the top of an old-fashioned dressing-table. Both David and I instantly saw what it had concealed and froze for the instant. The very thing that could have traced Matea's exact location was sitting right there. Her mobile phone, with the charging cable plugged into it, was placed centrally on the dressing-table top, surrounded by assorted perfume bottles, hairbrushes, jars and tubes of lotions. The cable ran to a socket in the wall and was still switched on.

'Bugger!' and that from a man who rarely swore. David swiftly disconnected the cable from the wall socket and put it and the phone into one of the plastic evidence bags, then into his pocket.

I looked into the wardrobe. Two suitcases were there, as were all the clothes that I remembered seeing her wear.

'Her thick navy jacket?' I asked, knowing Matea would have worn it in cold weather.

'Behind the back door. I'll go and see if it's still there,' offered Catherine, who turned and went downstairs. Meanwhile David was looking into drawers and along shelving, moving objects aside to see behind them. I did similarly, not really sure what I should be looking for.

'Any sign of her passport? The one we took all that trouble getting for her!' Mr Konstantinou had handed it over when David called on him following our so-called 'accident'.

'Also,' continued my copper spouse, 'see if you can find any stash of money. If not, she must have it all with her. I'll take her iPad, and give it a good looking-over. Just don't say a word about warrants to anyone!'

He carefully lifted the iPad from the top of the bedside cabinet and wrapped it, and the cable lying near it, with the black cardigan I had tossed onto the bed.

I found some small caches of money, a few £10 notes and some small change, nothing much, and no passport.

There were pictures posted on the wall: large-scale photographs of the Croatian countryside and coastline, posed publicity images of Justin Timberlake and Bradley Cooper, but many smaller print-outs of Matea selfies, smiling with others, most frequently Melissa and James. Some of these selfies I peeled off the wall and placed carefully in my plastic evidence bag. David nodded, approving.

Returning downstairs, we met a grim-faced Catherine.

'I can't find that jacket. It's not where she usually leaves it, behind the door. And I've looked everywhere else. Nowhere. Bother the girl! It looks like she actually walked out. Well, that's something I'll have words about with that Mr Konstantinou chap! Breaking a contract with no notice at all. And poor Melissa. She'll be devastated! Of course, maybe that bump on the head did it. She's not in her right mind.'

With that, I left to go home to organise something fairly instant for Sunday lunch with the Deanes. I hoped that Helena had it in hand, but could never be sure with her. David stayed on a few minutes to give his policemanish warning about driving with alcohol in the blood. He also made a point of asking for a list of everyone's name, address, and contact details, which James promised to provide that afternoon.

# Chapter 19

DAYS PASSED with no news. The American uncle received the email sent from Matea a few days before she went missing, but had heard nothing since. He promised to get in touch the moment he learned of anything.

Somehow the media got wind of the disappearance of the carer of the murder victim Ian Fletcher, and headlines began to appear in the local press, and then the nationals,

MISSING GIRL LINK TO MI5 MURDER

Stories carried only the main facts of the disappearance and nothing of the circumstances – drunken party, argument with boyfriend, and so on. The media acquired photographs of Matea, and with her appearance as a pretty, vivacious-looking young woman, they received massive exposure all over the media and the internet. Hashtags such as #missingMatea or #Croatianvictim began appearing and Twitters went wild with gossip. The *Huffington Post* managed to run internet pages of the story for days.

Speculation ran rife. The dark side of MI5 and GCHQ was once more paraded into full view. Historic rumours of possible clandestine authorised assassinations were regurgitated as fact, but more seemed to be drawn from James Bond fictions than reality.

Reporters began once more knocking on doors in the neighbourhood and asking intrusive questions about life in the sleepy village. There were even suggestions made in the *Mirror* and the *Sun* that Matea might have been in cahoots with the killer of Ian Fletcher. A Bonny-and-Clyde of espionage-based murder was grist to their mill.

Sue Roberts was on a high when she told us how once again she had rebuffed a reporter, this time one offering her a small fortune to reveal the low-down on the neighbours of the house where she 'did'.

'I told 'im straight where 'e could put 'is money! Never sez nuffin' about the party or how they wuz all pissed as newts. Nuffin' at all!'

Terri and I congratulated her on her discretion and we all enjoyed a few moments railing against the culture of media sensationalism.

Snide comments were made about the fact that the investigator of the murder lived in the very next house and yet could not prevent the abduction of the victim. These hurt, and although David shrugged them off, I could tell they rankled with him. He became quieter and more sombre, staying in the house as little as he could. Perhaps he feared being photographed on his days off doing something recreational and then being accused of playing while murders and were unresolved and young women went missing. Both the Fletchers' and the Deanes' door remained resolutely closed to the press, including the major television news companies.

Within a week or two the world's interest in the missing Matea story waned, and life went on.

The Christmas frenzy took its usual hold of the shops and the media had plenty of stories about that upon which to concentrate. The ubiquity of images and slogans of the 'perfect' Christmas Day, meal, and presents, sickened me. Smiling rosy-cheeked children and false snow, canned carols and happy-wishing cards.

All of it seemed so shallow, so pathetically trivial compared with the news broadcasts of wars and atrocities, accidents and murders. And the heart-breaking fact that our dear Matea was still missing. No word from her. No card or Christmas greeting.

It was a mood of solemn reality, not of seasonally manufactured joy, that set the scene for Christmas in the Deane house. We could not forget Matea, nor banish the fear of what might have happened to her. With great effort, all three Deanes and I made it to the Mass on Christmas Day, feeling our Croatian friend's absence keenly, as she would so have enjoyed the liturgy. I could barely restrain a tear during the carols.

Helena took a few days off around Christmas to visit

Ronald at his sister's in Bournemouth, and spent the festive period with them.

Catherine had taken James, Melissa and the three dogs away to a relative's soon after Matea's disappearance, arranging for the horses to be fed and watered in their absence. Apparently she has relatives who live in something approaching a stately home, and these people offered sanctuary during the media hysteria. They stayed there over Christmas, while calling back home from time to time to check on the house and the horses.

I could have done with Helena's help in the kitchen with the cooking on Christmas Day. She could have dealt with the large dead bird that the others expected, while I would have taken care of the 'top-of-the-range' nut-roast with plenty of chestnuts that I had selected as a treat. We all drank too much; even Tony was allowed a little for a change. Then, while Tony slept in his own bed, Terri, David and I snored in front of television, coming to only to toast the Queen during her Christmas message.

I could not wait for it all to be over and to get back to my researches. For me, immersion in my eighteenth-century literary and musical family, for I thought of the Burney family as a sort of alternative to my own, was not just escapism. For one thing it represented work, producing a book that I hoped would attract a new generation to Burney Studies. And that was important, because?

My answer was always two-fold. One, the literature in itself was worthy of examination and enjoyment. The novels, plays and journals of Fanny, the musical experiences of Dr Charles, the books of siblings such as Sarah Harriet and the potboilers of Elizabeth Meeke, all are rich with delight as well as being commentaries on the workings of the human heart, and secondly because the wealth of historical material, the different approaches to life of people just a few hundred years before us, gives us a perspective from which to discern and judge our own lives and world. High-minded reasons to work really hard.

Also, I could forget Matea – or try to.

# Chapter 20

DAVID'S MOROSE mood over Christmas, and general coldness towards me I put down to the same anxiety over Matea that I felt, adding to frustration over the unresolved murder case. He revived on the morning of his return to work on the Wednesday after Christmas, and even gave me a cheery peck on the cheek as he left the house. I thought, then, that was because he could occupy his mind with useful and hopefully fruitful work. Staff at the Gloucestershire police headquarters would be livelier than our morbid little household.

Oh well, time would tell.

Helena returned on the Friday of Christmas week and I was glad to see her. I never thought I would say that, but there,

I have. Ronald's sister had apparently made her stay there comfortable. She had been treated as an honoured guest and not allowed to set foot in the kitchen. The three of them had gone for bracing walks along the seafront and attended a couple of parties laid on by homes for the elderly. Sounded jolly. Not really my scene, but they enjoyed it. Maybe when I am their age...

The Fletchers returned on New Year's Day, and Helena and I went round to welcome them home and see that they had all they needed, as it was a Bank Holiday and a Sunday, so few stores would have been open.

The three dogs bounced around us, licking our hands and wagging energetically. Melissa greeted me with a warm hug, and then moved on to do the same to Helena. We all laughed with fondness at the girl's simple show of affection. Catherine politely asked after Terri and Tony, while James could barely restrain himself, blurting out,

'How're they going? Any news? Any further forward?'

He almost crumpled when we had to admit that we could not say, but that we had not heard anything to indicate where Matea might be. Melissa picked up on the sudden change of mood and began chanting 'Matea! Matea! Matea!'

Then she started crying and ran from the room, closely followed by James, intent on comforting her.

Helena and I declined the offer of tea, and returned home in silence, both reflecting on the enormity of the loss of Matea for both James and Melissa. At least, I assumed that was what occupied my mother's thoughts as they did mine.

\*\*\*\*

A few weeks into the new year, on a day of alternating sunshine and sharp heavy showers, I took lunch with Helena. She was feeling that Terri's constant negativity was getting her down, and she needed to see a cheerful face or go mad. To be fair to Terri, which I am not often, she was in almost constant pain, was stuck indoors with her ailing husband, and had little diversion. I tried pointing this out and Helena nodded, then declared,

'Well, I'm doing my best for her and never get any thanks. It wouldn't harm her to think of somebody else for a change.'

This from the most self-centred person I knew. Still, she was better company than Terri, and maybe she was becoming more considerate. I dreaded more of the 'love is everything' talk, and kept the conversation light.

After our light lunch, Helena faced the cold damp air outside to dig up some root vegetables from our cultivated patch near the tennis court while I sat at the desk. My concentration should have been focused on a reputed incestuous relationship within the Burney family, to which I gave no credence, but instead my thoughts kept returning to the missing Matea.

She was my friend, almost my own child, certainly not just an employee. Still there was not a word from her.

Just as I wrenched my attention back to the reputed scandal of Rear-Admiral James and his half-sister Sarah, Helena's face appeared at the study window. She rapped on the glass, so I leant over the desk to throw the window open.

.

'Yes?'

'Does James have a motor bike?'

'No, I'm sure he doesn't. Why?'

A cold dread tingled through me. Motorcycles round here do not herald good news.

'Well, I just saw a man run across his garden to the lane at the back, and heard a motorbike taking off.'

'God, Helena. Let's go. See what's happened. Run!'

I reached out for my mobile phone and raced outside, pounding down the drive with Helena just ahead.

I caught up with her as we arrived at the road. We turned together into the Fletchers's drive entrance and I ran as fast as the shingle allowed, just as I had that day when Ian was shot dead.

There was James' MiniCooper with the front passenger door wide open. James lay beside it on the grey pebbles with books and folders scattered around on the ground. He was moaning and writhing.

I caught up to him and leaned towards him, blurting out stupid questions, 'James, what happened? Are you all right? Have you been hurt? Where?'

He struggled to sit up, holding his lower right side, where blood was oozing between his fingers. Then his face blanched, his eyes rolled and he slumped back, unconscious but breathing.

Helena at once knelt beside him, taking off her quilted jacket to cover and warm him, and then she pressed down over the wound in a surprisingly efficient manner.

I was simply jabbing at the mobile and yelling for an ambulance when the cool voice of emergency services replied. I gave the address and urged speed as the victim had been shot or stabbed and was bleeding badly.

Next I rang David. He answered, sounding harassed, snapping, 'Yeah, what's up?'

'James has been attacked – shot or stabbed.'

'What? Where?'

'Here – outside his house. A motorcyclist made off down the lane at the back. Helena and I came round straight away. I've called an ambulance. He's still alive. Just.'

'I'll meet him at A & E, and I'll send round the CSIs and a forensic team right away. Stay where you are, unless the motorcyclist comes back. Don't disturb the scene too much. See you in a bit.'

I stayed as still as I could, waitingin the cold  for what seemed like aeons. After about a quarter of an hour I got up and went to the house. I tried the front door and the gun-room door on the off-chance they were unlocked. Then I shouted through doors and windows just in case someone was in and possibly in a slumber.

No one. The house was quiet. Catherine must have taken the dogs with her and Melissa was not expected home from college yet.

Was this attack on James linked to that on his father? It seemed so. There cannot be two murderous bikers intent on harming the Fletchers.

Was Matea's disappearance connected? Had she seen too much of the shooter's features for him to leave her alone? If not, where the hell was she? Had the same bastard who was trying to kill the Fletchers done something terrible to her? These thoughts swirled around my brain in confusion.

.

I found I was seething with anger, real fury, from my gut to my finger-tips. I wanted to find this motorcyclist and do him serious physical damage, especially if he knew where Matea was and if he was keeping her in some stinking tip.

I took some deep slow breaths and tried to attend to the beauty of the wintry scene around me: the bare branches of the willows and birches forming elaborate delicate tracery against the sky, the welcome green of the cypress trees and thickly berried holly bushes around the Fletchers' driveway and entrance.

Calmer and steadier, I relieved Helena of the job of pressing down over the wound to limit the blood loss. She stood up and abstractedly put her hands over her face to wipe away sweat or tears, leaving blood staining her cheeks and with drops even falling down the front of her jumper.

James' eyes flickered as he began to regain consciousness, but I told him to lie still, not move and to keep his eyes closed and try to relax. He did as instructed, and his breathing became more measured and less laboured.

Then the ambulance arrived and professional hands took over from ours.

Following closely after the paramedics were the police, arriving in a convoy of marked and unmarked cars. After telling them all we saw and knew, we were allowed to go home.

# Chapter 21

OVER AN HOUR after we had found James's stricken body, David arrived. He strode into the living room, where we had both crashed onto comfortable chairs. I was unable to work or even read as thoughts and theories were again coursing around my brain, suggesting one scenario after another.

Helena had poured us both a whisky and we were chatting aimlessly about trivia and nonsense, interspersed with sudden interjections of 'Oh God!' or 'Why? What could James possibly have done to deserve that?'

Just as David entered, Helena took a phone call on her

mobile. She put her hand over the receiver to mouth to us, 'It's Catherine'.

She agreed to whatever Catherine was asking, then stood up and made for the door, explaining, 'Catherine wants me to meet Melissa off the Star College bus and bring her here. She doesn't want her to know what's happened to James, so I'll go over there now as it won't be long. Poor girl, she'll be expecting James to see to her while her mummy's out. I'll have to think of something. See you later.'

David then explained that he had called in to see James at the A&E and left when Catherine arrived. She had been, in her own 'stiff-upper-lip' way, distraught, even quite tearful. James's face was covered with an oxygen mask, and he had been in no condition to be interviewed.

While I was telling David everything I knew, from the moment of Helena's knock at the window right up to the ambulance arriving, we could hear the door opening and closing and Helena's voice inviting Melissa into the kitchen. She and Helena were soon singing something and laughing. I was so pleased that the girl was blithely unaware of the latest family drama. My mother was becoming rather good at distracting Melissa. Good for Mum.

Did I say that?

David asked me to show him where I had found James, so I threw on a warm jacket and we went round to the Fletchers'. A police vehicle was parked in the driveway and David spoke through the window to its occupant. Apparently she was a forensic investigator, and had just completed her work there. She then backed her car down to the road, and went off.

I pointed to the place on the shingle, next to the now-closed car door, where the boy had lain. A small pool of dark dry blood marked the spot. The books had been tidied up and placed in a pile on the passenger seat. We then crossed the garden and went through the low wooden gate into the lane.

David peered at the ground and followed tyre tracks in the mud until they petered out on stonier ground. He scooped up a morsel of the mud with a pen and smeared it into a plastic evidence bag he had withdrawn from his pocket. Curious horses kept up with us on the other side of the hedge. The low golden light gave a beauty and peace to the rural scene at odds with the human activity recently enacted nearby.

'I'd like to see James again. I'm going back to the A&E. I couldn't speak to him when I called in before.' These were first words David had uttered since we trekked the lane.

'Me too. I'll come with you.'

He knew arguing was useless, so we walked back up to our house and put our heads round the kitchen door to say goodbye to Helena and to ask her to look in on Terri and Tony. Melissa greeted us with a happy wide smile. I then went inside the kitchen to the larder and picked up a chocolate bar and a banana to snack on just in case that would have to replace or put off a proper meal that evening. David wanted just a banana.

We were a few miles from the house driving down the A38 towards Gloucester when David took a call, and put it on speaker. He stopped the car to take the details, noting them in a pocket jotter. A woman's voice with a slight West Country burr spoke.

'DI Deane? Sergeant Wood here. Good news from the

ANPR camera sightings, sir. We've picked up a suspect motorbike going south along the A38 just over an hour or so ago. Then it seems to have disappeared after entering the village of Norton – no further sightings. But we have followed a few high-sided vehicles, including a couple of horse-boxes, which could have collected and stashed the bike on one of the little side roads. One box in particular, Sir,  seems a real possibility.'

'Go on, sounds promising.'

'It was picked up on the A4123 going West. It is an unmarked horse-box heading down nearly an hour ago on the M50 towards Ross. It is the only horse-box which has no stable marked on it that we can check for alibis. We have checked those others and they all seem to have good reasons for being where they were. Now we've got it again, it's beyond Ross on the A40, sir. Seems it stopped to refuel. Probably going to Abergavenny. It's going rather fast if carrying horses.'

'Put out a road block, if you can. Stop that vehicle! Check it out. No, don't stop it! It could contain an armed suspect. Repeat, he could be armed. Call the Gwent Police, get permission to pursue and see if they can get on its trail. Is the Chief OK with this? Have you told him?'

'Yes, sir. He says we're to do whatever you say; he'll back you up,'

David came alive; his eyes glistened. He turned to me as he started up the engine, and spoke quickly with excitement.

'This could be a real break! I'll run you home and then go after this horse-box. James will have to wait.'

'Never mind about running me home. I'm coming with you. I mean it! You can't waste the time for one thing. Go!'

The journey excited me; I could feel my heart beating faster. At last, perhaps, there would be an answer to the riddle of Matea's disappearance, and why the Fletcher men have been targeted.

Like on a sinister treasure hunt we went from sighting to sighting, informed along the route by officers stationed in Gloucester. We took the A40 going west at Gloucester and joined the route of the horse-box where the M50 peters out into the A40 and turns towards the south west.

When we moved into another county, another country even, and a different police authority, a furious verbal transaction took place requesting permission to pursue the suspect vehicle. It had too much of a head start for us to physically catch it up, or for a road block to be viable, even if it were safe, but the information from the road cameras, the ANPRs, and from police observers along the route kept a steady stream of information to enable us to pursue it.

I was amazed and somewhat alarmed that there were so many eyes along the road. How very Big Brother. But David assured me that only very few officers had access to the information gleaned from them and only for specific projects such as this one.

You might gain a picture of where these cameras are, or are not, he explained, if you follow several investigations of incidents in the same area, but that would be unusual. Some magistrates and lawyers may make such a mental map from local cases where tracking has been used in evidence.

But the public and most of the police themselves remain unaware of how much potential surveillance there is around, even on country roads. Their value in tracking specific vehicles, within very tight controls, is really high, according to David.

They might be located at approaches to villages or at crossroads or mounted upon traffic lights. But as they cost thousands of pounds each, depending on whether they are monitored or simply containing recording equipment, most cash-strapped rural police forces use them sparingly.

The horse-box driver was obviously one who was unaware that his journey was being followed, as the trail led directly to a farm south of Raglan in Monmouthshire.

In just over an hour from leaving the house, we joined several other police vehicles waiting for us at the end of a long farm track. David got out and spoke with some of the personnel in the other cars. Then he and they got back into their vehicles and we all drove in single file along the muddy track the horse-box had travelled not long before. With all headlights off, the convey used only moonlight to guide it.

As the lane approached the house, it widened out until there was sufficient room for our car to turn around to face the road and for the others quietly to park randomly between the farmhouse and a dry stone wall which ran the length of the lane and back beyond the house. David unbelted himself and was about to leave when he turned to me, index finger on his lips, and insisted that I stay in the car and not do anything, nor say anything.

'Can I even think?'

'Yes, do that.' Irony is lost on David. 'And keep your eyes open. Keep my speed-dial number under your thumb for anything you need to tell me about that you see from the car.'

He got out and closed the door silently, then joined a

cluster of other officers, some wearing bullet-proof jackets and carrying standard-issue firearms.

I had to strain to see during the times when the nearly full moon disappeared behind a cloud, but otherwise, by twisting round in my seat, I had a good view of the action to my left. The officers mutely gestured instructions to each other, most of them converging on the front of the farmhouse, others hurrying around towards the back of the building.

The brick-built Victorian house was the sort that young children draw, with a central door, four windows and chimneys on the roof. This one had a fair amount of ivy growing up it, and the sagging slate roof looked in need of repair. From the far side of it and across the yard from where I was stationed, spread a series of ramshackle sheds and outhouses.

There were lights on in the downstairs rooms of the house, and by unclouded moonlight, I could see quite clearly as David and his colleagues furtively approached the front door. One of the police officers must have found it unlocked, for it was flung wide open and he went inside, yelling 'Police! Armed officers! Stand still!' He was followed immediately by the others. Much shouting ensued for a moment, then all went quiet and the door was closed.

I lost interest after a few moments staring at the dark doorway, and my neck was beginning to ache from twisting round. So I panned along the outbuildings to my left, wondering what each contained. As my gaze reached the last shed, the one furthest from the house, I noticed a dark figure emerging and running towards me.

Oh my God! I froze for a moment, and in panic

considered whether to stay in my present position in order to watch his progress, or duck down and hope he did not see me. While dithering, he, for the silhouetted figure seemed indubitably male, crouching over as he ran, seemed to be aiming not at my car itself but at a point behind it on the stone wall, the one to my right which ran alongside the length of the lane.

He was getting nearer! My heart was pounding and I held my breath. Instinct caused me to lower myself and turn my face away from the window. I heard his footsteps, quick and soft on the stony ground, as he hurried past.

Now what to do? I rose in the seat and turned to watch through the rear window. He was jogging alongside the wall for a few yards, then turned into an opening in it. Whether he had hidden behind the wall or was running in one direction or another I could not tell.

David! I must call him. Either that or yell. But calling out loud might bring the runner back to the car if he was still nearby. Scary thought. I fumbled for the speed dial number, noticing how my hands were shaking with fear and excitement. There was prolonged silence, no calling tone. I could just make out from the tiny icon that the signal was missing. Still silence.

What was I to do? Stay still and let the fugitive escape? By the time I ran to the house the man would be far gone in any direction. By crossing the yard I would make a target of myself if he was armed and watching.

Of course, what I had to do was, very quietly, follow the wall to the opening and see where the figure had gone. If I kept out of sight and controlled my breathing I could sense whether or not he was close at hand or had run off. Then I could try for a better signal to let David know where he was heading, or run to the house, or call out loud.

Nothing else for it. With my heart beating fast and an overwhelming sense of exhilaration, I turned off the interior light that activates when a door is opened, got out of the car, leaving the door ajar.

I followed the wall along, as close as I could get to it, picking my steps out stealthily among the nettles and grasses.

When I was a child, my friends and I amused ourselves by following a randomly-selected member of the public along the street, pretending we were police following a suspect. We tried to remain unseen, should the 'suspect' turn around, by darting into doorways and creeping sideways along walls. We were stalkers, except we did not know that term, or that it was an offence. It was harmless childish fun. I felt that I was playing that same game now, only for real.

# Chapter 22

I SLOWED AS I approached the dark opening through which I had seen the figure pass through the wall.

I held my breath, and even pulled in my stomach, as I inched nearer, listening intently to any sound of another person's presence. Every nerve in my body was tense and alert.

Nothing. The only noise was from occasional traffic on the distant road, night owls hooting to each other and further away a fox barking. I exhaled slowly, watching my breath form a little cloud before my mouth, and crept along to where a metal-tubed gate was swinging open on its hinges. The grassy verge at the foot of the wall gave way to sticky mud, and large clear footprints pointed away from the house. I glooped through the mud, carefully, so as not to slip on it, and could make out a field rising to a hill, occupied by a few grazing sheep, and trees forming a sort of screen on the skyline on the crest of the hill in the distance.

I tried the phone again, cupping my hands round it so that the light from it did not show and so that I could talk into it quietly. This time the connection worked as David straightaway answered, 'Yes?'

I was just about to speak when, Wham!

My arm exploded with pain. Something hard and heavy struck it with great force just above the elbow. I shrieked as the phone shot from my hand and landed somewhere on the ground.

A pair of strong hands covered my mouth and throat, and warm breath hit the back of the neck.

'Bitch!' the voice behind me hissed. Sheer terror coursed through me, adrenalin pumping in overload.

The man's knee thumped hard against the back of my right leg, knocking me off balance. At the same time his hand left the grip on my throat and struck across the back of my shoulders, forcing me forward and downwards, face into the mud.

With his left hand pressing down on the back of my head while he groped on the ground for my phone with his right hand, my gasps for air forced my nostrils and mouth into taking in tasteless draughts of slimy mud. I could have choked right there, only all of a sudden, he released me.

By turning my head, I saw him pick up an object, my mobile phone I realised, and throw it far into the distance. Then he stood up. Delivering a forceful kick at my prone body, near my throbbing elbow, he took off across the field towards the line of trees. I just lay there, gasping, as if movement would be more dangerous than the chill I would likely catch from the cold damp Winter earth beneath me.

In a moment I heard shouts and my name being called from the direction of the house. I pulled myself up into a kneeling position, miserable, cold and shivering. What had possessed me to follow a fugitive, one who may well have been armed? This was likely to be the assassin of Ian and would-be killer of James.

Was this man involved in Matea's disappearance too?

Had I come *so close* to finding out all the answers? If only I had been in a  position to ask the questions and receive the knowledge I craved. I felt the tears close to my eyelids.

What made my stomach then suddenly lurch was apprehension at the inevitable accusations of stupidity and worse that David would justifiably level at me. I  could hear his voice calling my name.

'Here, over here,' I gathered the energy to call back, rising, unsteadily, to my feet from the sticky, glutinous mud.

David and two others appeared at the gateway. As I fell into my partner's outstretched arms, he directed the others to pursue the escapee.

'Over there…' I gestured vaguely towards the tree-line in the distance. Two young plainclothes officers set off running.

David then pushed me away, looking down in fastidious horror at the mud now transferred onto his jacket. He looked back into my face as if at some strange alien being.

'What the hell…?'

'Don't start, please, David. You didn't pick up. The signal was poor, so when I saw him run, I followed to see where he went. I wasn't going to confront him, or anything…'

'I should bloody hope not! But that is what it seems

you have done! Where is the phone now? Wait, I'll ring it.'

We picked up the faint sound of my mobile's signal. Eventually we found it, by which time I had stopped shaking quite so dramatically, but still felt nauseous. And embarrassed. And stupid.

I accompanied David meekly across the yard and into the farm house. Once inside he pointed to the kitchen sink. I went over to it, turned on the cold water tap and flushed out my mouth, spitting out the gritty mud. I then splashed fresh water over my face, scraping off patches of damp Welsh soil and possibly cow or sheep dung. After some moments, I regained sufficient composure to turn towards the roomful of Welsh police officers and whoever else was there.

A small grey-haired man with a red, weathered face and dark chin stubble, was sitting at the wooden kitchen table, with four strapping uniformed officers standing near him.

Before him on the table in a clear plastic bag was a handgun complete with silencer. Everyone just bided their time, silently.

As the noisy kitchen clock ticked out the minutes, the man took out from a trouser pocket a tin of tobacco and a small green folder of Rizla papers, and rolled a cigarette.

'I can smoke in my own bloody home, can't I?' he scowled. The officers simply shrugged and shuffled their feet. They were all broad shouldered, well set-up young men, two wearing bullet-proof jackets over their uniforms. The local rugby squad must recruit from the cops round here.

A few minutes later, police numbers in this rural kitchen were augmented by another burly young uniformed male officer, and the first woman I had seen in this company.

·

She was short but forbidding-looking, a plain-clothed officer who spoke with a distinctly Welsh accent. With her starkly pulled-back hair, expressionless face and no-nonsense attitude I decided she must be a dragon to work with, and pitied her colleagues. She read from a spiral-bound notepad, reporting an inventory of the sheds and outbuildings.

'Four motorbikes, Sir, all on racks, one being a sport type, motorcross vehicle, about ten years old, with wet mud still on the tyres. The three others look newer and with parts missing, including one top-of-the-range black Honda. Several number plates lying around, Sir, probably all stolen.'

'Or salvaged – we'll check them out. Anything else?'

'Not of interest, Sir, but some of our lads will go through them in the morning. We'll check out the mud on the tyres with the soil-type in the lane behind your house, Sir.'

She held up the plastic bag into which David had earlier scraped mud from the lane. Now I saw its significance.

David introduced his wayward wife to DS Donna Price and I smiled sheepishly while this self-possessed young woman returned a glare. David and she then talked on about procedure, while I withdrew attention in order to focus on my throbbing injuries. I hoped my arm and ribs had not been broken, but the pain was intense. I was given a chair and sat miserably, rubbing my arm and side and wanting above all to go home. Voices murmured indistinctly around me and the farmer's tobacco smoke added another layer of unpleasantness to the already musty atmosphere. It was still early evening, but I felt very tired.

After a period of dragging time, other voices drew closer and I started into wakefulness as the door clattered open.

Two young men in casual clothes entered, dragging between them a third man in muddy worn jeans and a torn denim jacket. He had the bushiest dark eyebrows and blackest moustache and beard that I had ever seen on a young man. I almost expected him to pull them off with a 'Tirrah!', but he was in no mood for jokes. He was hobbling, lifting up his right foot from the ground, and swearing curses on the forces of law on either side of him.

'Here he is, Sir. Gave himself up when he sprained his ankle running from us. Not armed, Sir. Or nothing found on him. Not said a word.'

'What's your name?' barked David in a tone of such aggression I hardly believed it came from him. 'We'll find out soon enough, so don't waste our time.'

'Go on, O'Neill. You might as well tell the bastards,' the man at the table helpfully contributed. A real 'Don't tell them, Pike' moment.

'Thomas O'Neill,' muttered the captive.

David arrested him on suspicion of murder and of attempted murder and recited the caution. The man spluttered, denying knowing anything about anything.

'Say nothing,' commanded his friend. 'Don't tell the bastards anything!'

'I'll arrest this one,' offered DS Price, glaring at the farmer. 'I'll bring him over to Gloucester and in the morning we'll go over this place with a forensics team. See what shows up about the gun and the bikes.'

David thanked her and left her cautioning the farmer while he phoned through to Superintendent Locke in Gloucester, apologising for disturbing him and recounting the salient points of the two arrests. He then turned to O'Neill.

'We'll get you to the station in  Gloucester where your ankle will be seen by a doc and we'll get  you a brief.  OK? Well,  how about a "sorry" to my wife for pushing her in the mud?'

Nothing but a glare from O'Neill, but definitely suppressed titters from the policemen. I was beyond caring.

Apart from a couple of uniformed officers deputed to seal the house and sheds with tape after we had left, the rest of us went with the prisoners and drove off in  a convey of cars, most of the Gwent Police vehicles peeling off after a few miles. Two were  left, following ours, carrying the prisoners with officers to guard them.

David and I travelled largely in silence. I could tell he was furious with me, and I spent the first part of the journey angrily inventing justifications for my crazy actions that I could use if he again questioned them.

As we were approaching Gloucester I had calmed down and felt just embarrassment. My arm and ribs still ached, but of course the danger could have been even greater had my attacker been armed or had wanted to kill me. At this thought, my indignation with David's negativity weakened. By the time we reached the business park near Gloucester where the police have their headquarters, I was wanting almost abjectly to crave his forgiveness. That would have to be acted upon later.

At the custody centre behind the HQ and across the road from Prism House, David gave one of young officers the keys to his car and instructions to take me home and then report back.

'Don't wait up,' he said to me grimly. He then strode

off to the first marked police car carrying one of the prisoners, leaving me, mortified, miserable, and hurting, in the company of a taciturn young man who simply did as he was told.

# Chapter 23

I WOKE NEXT MORNING in the thin light of dawn, disturbed by the sound of the hall door closing. David was returning after a long night of questioning the prisoner. He thoughtfully crashed out on the long sofa in the sitting room for a couple of hours rather than wake me. By the time we were seated at the kitchen table with coffee and toast before us, it was already mid-morning.

He, with eyes puffy with lack of sleep, kept his concentration on his smartphone, tapping in letters and reading intently whatever it displayed. I was at a loss as to how to break the ice. Do I apologise, or pretend last night did not happen? Eventually, my nerves were so taut I had to speak. David could hold out for ever. Not me.

'Look, David. I'm sorry, all right? Can we put it behind us and carry on? Otherwise …'

Without taking his eyes off his device, which I took as meaning that he could not even bear to look at me, he replied,

'Yes, of course. I'm sorry too. I should never have left

you there in the car alone. I should never have taken you at all. How's the arm?'

I told him it still hurt, but that my looks had improved for having received a facial mud pack of wet Welsh soil and dung. He grinned. After that, to my relief, we were able to move on to the enquiry. He turned his phone off, pocketed it and after a few deep breaths answered my first question which was, naturally, about Matea.

'No luck there. If he knows, he's not saying. Don't worry, the Gwent Police are trawling through every item in his crib and we'll go over every moment of his miserable life.'

That was little comfort.

'However, we've got enough on him to connect him to James's wounding and hopefully he'll cough to Ian Fletcher's murder.'

He paused to tell me that he had heard James was out of danger and on the mend. The bullet apparently had not passed through any significant organ and had caused little internal damage. It seems James had knocked the lengthy silencer aside, so disturbing the aim of the gunman.

'From what we've learnt, this Thomas O'Neill is the son of a bloke called Michael O'Neill, or that's the name he took up after the Troubles. That was his second name, I mean the second one he was known by.'

'How come?'

'Well, according to my MI5 contact, someone originally called Fergus Curran was turned by Ian Fletcher from being just a Republican sympathiser, involved in low-level sabotage, into becoming a Super Grass for the British.'

'How? How did Fletcher do that, I've always

.

wondered what would make someone turn around so completely?'

'By the use of blackmail and threats, apparently. Fighting dirty in a filthy war. Fletcher gave him a handler who saw to it that this Curran bloke got in thick with some top IRA types.'

'So, why should that now…?'

'Hold on. Curran passed on quite a bit of good Intel. Apparently saved more than a few lives and screwed up a couple of major bombings. Should have had a medal, really.'

'Really?'

'Yes, brave work, when you think of it. However, it seems that after the Good Friday Peace Agreement he was just dropped. Left out to dry, as they like to say. No great effort to save his identity or give him extra security. So, you can imagine, he really got it in the neck when they worked out who'd been grassing them up.'

'What happened to him?'

'Well, when his flimsy cover was blown – name change, new address, that was about it – some of the comrades he'd been betraying to our lot picked him up one day, did him in and left his tortured remains where his son would find them, on the road where the lad did his paper round. So you see, our O'Neill is a rather screwed up young man, well, not so young any more. All that happened nearly twenty years ago. Added to which, the mother, O'Neill's, died of a heart attack shortly after. That left O'Neill thirsting for the blood of the MI5 guy who set his father up. And that, of course, is Ian Fletcher, lately of GCHQ but formerly of MI5.'

'What took him so long? And why now?'

'That we don't know, but maybe he got wind that old Fletcher was dying and thought that if he didn't act soon, he'd miss his chance. Maybe it just took a long time to find out who was behind his father's handler. After all, people are now writing candid memoirs and giving TV interviews about their work in the secret services. That was all hush-hush at one time.'

'Why didn't he go after the thugs who killed his father? And who's the farmer whose house you stormed last night? What had he got to do with it?'

David was relaxed now and seemed to be enjoying relating the facts. By telling me, he used to say, he could sort out and clarify the facts in his mind. Apparently, so he said, my questions helped him to prepare his reports and get his ideas in order.

'Question one – don't know. Who can say, unless he feels he has more in common with them than with us? Or maybe he has already, or was planning to after taking out the man at the top. Question two – that farmer, Hugh Williams, has harboured a grudge against the English since the time of Owen Glendower. He even positively loathes the Welsh Assembly. He calls it an English plot to keep the Welsh a subject people.

'That nice DS last night gave him quite a grilling. He's now been transferred to Gwent HQ at Newport and says he'll only answer further questions in Welsh. He has been charged with conspiracy. We were thinking of joint enterprise, but we've got to be careful with that one. It seems he had supplied the motorcycles and false plates, and the horse-box as the getaway vehicle, while O'Neill provided the firearm and ammo. Two lonely, disgruntled men feeding each other with anti-English propaganda until they were ready to kill.'

'Poor James, he wasn't responsible for what his father did! Why pick on him?'

'No, but maybe the son of the victim felt it only right that Fletcher's son should suffer too. Perhaps he never meant to kill him, just show him what hate looks like.'

'But why abduct Matea, if that's what they have?'

'We don't know that they did. I'll be checking their stories for the time she took off.'

'If that's what she did…'

# Chapter 24

AFTER A SHOWER and shave, David took himself off to work, but without giving me the customary cursory kiss. I still felt largely unforgiven. Or unloved. Well, less loved. Something.

I sat there after he left, brooding on his behaviour towards me, not just that morning, but for weeks past. There was nothing tangible. Nothing more than a slight feeling of chill between us, whereas before, in the London days, we had enjoyed a real warmth and good humoured intimacy, physical and emotional. Since moving West, that has been slowly dissipating. I could tell that making love in his parents' house was inhibiting. That I could understand.

And, at our age, we no longer needed to be going at it like we used to, like a couple of lively rabbits, he would joke. But there was something of a lessening in other expressions and demonstrations of closeness. How long ago was it since he put his

146

arm around me affectionately? Or since I caught him out looking at me fondly with that hint of a smile?

Of course, all marriages go through stages, I know that. We cannot keep up the honeymoon for years. Maybe we were just lucky that it seemed to last so long in our case, and now after eleven years of married life I should perhaps expect everything to slow down and cool. What was it Hilary Clinton said in her autobiography? Something about, meeting Bill when they were both students, they 'started a conversation' – 'and we're still talking', or some such.

Certainly I've seen married couples sitting together for hours on end, in restaurants or on trains and they were not talking. Not even passing little comments, little observations, to each other. But David and I had always been talkers, always sharing what was on our minds, what the day had brought, what we felt about this and that. Until now. These days not only is less spoken between us, but we are not even making much eye contact.

Maybe not arguing is a good thing. We always did plenty of that – occasionally violently raised voices, usually just spats and disagreements. (Making up afterwards used to be good). But now we seem to be just keeping our own counsel. He tells me less about cases and colleagues, and I have little to share other than about what I have been reading and discovering about the brilliant eighteenth-century family of Burneys. I could not share much at all after he recently told me not to bore him about books he would never read and people in whom he had no interest. That hurt more deeply than he knew, although I indicated my feelings as well as I could by the strictly silent routine for a whole day. He scarcely noticed.

Like his mother, he felt he was above the sort of village gossip I gleaned from Sue Roberts, which I enjoyed immensely although it was rarely salacious, and I did not trouble him with sharing Helena's views on life. They were best left unrepeated.

Was that healthy? Was it me? Had I changed? Well, maybe I was less fun, less interesting. Less warm to him, perhaps? In the London days I would leave work behind, or that world of people anyway, and return to a different setting. Maybe commuting made a difference, created a necessary barrier between work and home, even though we both brought work home at times. But now, for me, work and home are merged into one. Maybe I'd become a lonely bore and drove David to finding stimulation elsewhere? I did not know, and was troubled.

With whom could I talk this over? Certainly not Helena, the scourge of convention who would like nothing better than our marriage to fall apart. Not Terri, not only because she could only ever see things from the viewpoint of her beloved son, but also because she is such a darned misery. Tony, no. He's so old-school that he would not know where to begin discussing feelings and relationships. Matea? Oh, dear missing girl – not that she's old enough. Catherine? She'd tell me to 'pull myself together' or something similar.

Bugger it! Why did I ever agree to leave colleagues and friends behind just to satisfy the filial duties of the husband about whose love I was now beginning to question. Was I becoming bitter and resentful? Oh well, better get back to work. Delving into the lives of an intriguing and fascinating bunch of historical, even historic, people was more satisfying than pondering on those of twenty-first century ones with the power to hurt.

I worked intensely in my study for most of the day, reading and making notes, apart from short walks in the garden to clear my head. In the late afternoon I slumped on a chair in the sitting room to revise a version of what I had been writing.

At about seven, David returned. After he and I took a light

meal in the kitchen, he invited Terri, Helena and me into the sitting room to brief us on the investigation.

We settled comfortably, whisky glasses in hand, then he began.

'We can discard the killer of Ian, or at least the wounder of James, from the picture.'

I did not need him to explain what picture. Matea was always on our mind. He continued.

'Their alibis check out for the night Matea disappeared. The Welsh guy was at A&E in Abergavenny getting a nasty cut from a farming machine looked at. He was there from 8pm until past midnight. O'Neill was bonking some woman – sorry, Mother – he'd picked up in a club in Belfast. We identified him on the club's CCTV. One than actually works! When our colleagues in Belfast questioned her she had no difficulty remembering him. Apparently, they spent the night together and the next day he had taken her to some swanky restaurant for Sunday lunch. He had told her he was a wealthy property developer, or something. He encouraged her to order the best food on the menu and the most expensive wine. While waiting for coffee, he said he just needed to go to the gents – went out and never came back, leaving her with a horrendous bill to pay! Said she'd never forget his cheating face, and picked him out right away.'

We laughed at the poor woman's naiveté. What a cheap trick.

'So now,' David's face then fell into his serious look. 'That rather throws attention on two other, separate, lines of enquiry. The Konstantinou mystery of what was going on in the farm shed that so spooked Matea, and whether being run off the road was associated with that. That's one. But we've nothing on the man. His books have been trawled through and his agency carers all speak of his fair dealings with them.

That leaves the Croatian-Serb connection. If the Northern Irish Troubles can still cause acts of revenge and retaliation, so presumably can the just-as-murderous Balkan wars.'

I mused over that point. It seemed entirely reasonable, if horrible. How can people hold grudges after so long a time? Do wars ever really end in peace? I remembered Nana Ivy saying that when she went on her first visit to Germany, when she was the age I am now, World War Two had been over for twenty years, but she still felt moments of bitter resentment against the whole German race. She knew such feelings were shameful, if perhaps understandable.

David was looking at me, impatient with my reverie.

'Julia, are you with me? Anyway…d'you know what the gunman said as he shot James? "Justice!", that's what. That what James told us. Though how that can be any kind of justice! Trying to kill or even just wound a kid who was only a toddler when the Good Friday Agreement was signed, I don't know.'

'So did they confess to the killing and wounding?'

'Not exactly. It'll have to go to trial. They both expressed how they would like to have done it, but tried to put the blame on other people. According to them, there were queues of people ready to take a shot at Ian Fletcher. O'Neill, with pressure from his lawyer, did fess up to the wounding of James, and said that was inspired by the killing of the boy's father, although that was something he had not done. The evidence is overwhelming. He could not get out of that. But it was a different gun used for the father's murder, so we still do not have enough to clinch that one yet. Maybe there was another person involved. There was a name they both gave, a Robbie Walsh, and we're checking on that right now. My Super is flying over to Belfast to follow up that lead, if it is one. He's taking a couple of others from the squad, but I don't need to go. I want to follow the other line of enquiry'

'What's that?'

'I'm thinking of going to Croatia. Check out Matea's family background – that "father" that the note mentioned. It might just help. Who knows, she may even be there, sitting at home like nothing happened!'

'In that case I'm coming with you – I know, the last time I said that wasn't entirely brilliant, but before you try to stop me, you owe me a holiday! I know this won't be much of a vacation as such, but a change of scene will do me good and I'll think I'm doing something about finding Matea. Of course, I'll pay my way, so you can you can't really stop me.'

# Chapter 25

THE FOLLOWING SUNDAY morning David and I were sitting on a Croatian airline flight from Heathrow to Zagreb. The flight had been delayed an hour as snow had to be cleared from the runway at Zagreb. I worried about catching our onward flight, but the smaller plane had obligingly awaited our arrival as most of the other passengers and crew were also transferring. We landed at Dubrovnik and, with only cabin luggage, were clear of passport control by five o'clock, local time. A smartly dressed young woman was standing in the arrivals hall holding up a card with 'D.I. David Deane' on it. We converged on her, and she introduced herself as Lucy, and what sounded like 'Babitch'. She was the honorary consul, an Englishwoman married to a Croatian.

She led us to a nearby airport café to tell us some important late developments. I was amazed that a coffee cost just about a pound, and glasses of iced water were brought to the table as well. Lucy, as she asked us to call her, was pleasant and friendly, with a natural efficiency that made every task look effortless. We talked about the journey, and then to the point.

'David, you asked the police to look for the family of Matea Pilić at the address she had given to her employer' – looking at her notes – 'and he is a Mr Konstantinou?'

'Well, he runs the agency. She was employed by our neighbours, and by us.'

'OK, I see. Well, that address was here in Dubrovnik. But when I went there with our detective, after getting your call, there was no-one there. The house was locked up and neighbours say that Mr Pilić, the girl's father, had left suddenly, a couple of weeks ago. They said that he took off in his car with boxes of goods and told them that he did not know when or if he would be returning. He left no forwarding address. Just gave the key to his neighbour to give to the landlord. He said he would post the outstanding rent. We checked with the landlord who said everything had been settled and his lease terminated.'

She looked up at David's face which was registering both annoyance and disappointment.

'But,' she smilingly added (the little tease), 'the police in Split have reported his turning up there. They found him this morning, while you were flying here. So, although I should have enjoyed having your company here for a few days, I suggest you go to Split tomorrow. I'll make the arrangements. Meanwhile, please, both of you, come to the hotel I have booked for you, and I'll pick you up later to take you to my house for dinner. Unless you'd prefer to eat out?'

She looked from one to the other. David accepted her offer with alacrity. I screwed up my face with concern, and informed her that as a vegetarian, I should hate to put her to any trouble. She waved that aside as 'no bother at all' and led us to her smart black Mercedes, waiting on the airport forecourt car-park. I loved seeing palm trees there in January, so evocative of warm summer days.

She drove us to a parking space outside the Ploče Gate set into the amazingly intact and impressive walls of the old city, and led us on foot the short journey through narrow streets into the old city. We trundled our small wheeled cases over the cobbles to the main square and to the Pucić Palace Hotel. She preceded us into the small lobby, and negotiated our registration with the smart, good-looking receptionist. I swore he winked at me. After shaking hands, she offered to collect us from there at seven o'clock.

Later that evening, we were eating a mushroom ragout over polenta slices. This was taken with a Croatian Chardonnay from the Domaine Koquelicot, and was followed by a poppy-seed strudel, heavy on the cinnamon and with generous amounts of apricot jam. We ate this with a sweet desert Prošek. It was all delicious.

I look round admiringly at the honorary consul's spacious apartment in the suburbs of the city. Everything was expensive-looking and tasteful; nothing out of place, no jarring colours or objects. Certainly no piles of half-read magazines and junk-mail flyers that 'might be interesting'. Flowers, blooming colourfully even in January, adorned the larger surfaces, and Impressionist paintings that were probably authentic originals, graced the walls.

Lucy, who had cooked the meal herself, still looking immaculate, explained that her husband was an MEP, and spent much of his time in Brussels. The arrangement suited her fine, as she was able to pursue her consulate work with few interruptions. Winter was quiet as few tourists visited the tiny city at this season – unlike the hordes of them clogging up the streets and squares in the summer months.

'The worst', she said with a noticeable shudder, 'are the giant cruise ships that disgorge literally thousands of people, all at the same time, and make movement around the city impossible. They can see nobody but others from their ship, and take in nothing of the life and culture of the people here. Of course, they buy their tacky souvenirs and buy drinks in the bars, but do not really contribute to the economy. And certainly not to the quality of life here. Some do not even seem to know what country they are in!'

We clucked and nodded. 'At least,' she continued, they are usually not here long enough to bother my office – unless they miss their ship and are too drunk to remember what it is called!'

David then brought up the subject of the Balkan Wars and we discussed the devastation that had been caused in Dubrovnik and elsewhere, and the horrors of ethnic cleansing. Then she delivered an item of information that had us riveted.

'You know the man you are looking for – Josip Pilić – is a war criminal?'

Our eyes widened.

'The police here have been looking into his background since you first told us that his daughter went missing and you could not contact him. They found out that he was one of the commanders of a Croatian unit that slaughtered a number of unarmed Serb and Muslim prisoners and civilians. He was known as Josip-Mario Penić' in those days, and changed his name to Pilić' about twenty years ago, presumably to protect his family.'

Another name changed for protection. I was beginning to doubt anybody's was the one they were born with.

'So Matea might not have known about his background?'

'Mmm, it's possible. Although he is a hero in some circles, most people even here regard his actions, especially the killing of women and children, as beyond the pale. There were revenge killings by the enemy, as you'd imagine, and his name was often used as the reason for them.'

'What happened to Matea's mother? Did she die of cancer, as Matea believes?'

'Yes, that's true, according to hospital records.'

'And the young man Luka, do you know about him? Matea called him a friend of the family.'

'That must be Luka Tušek. That's another case. His father and Matea's were comrades. Commanded a similar unit and involved in similar atrocities. The two men are still close and the son, Luka, is a younger version of his father. Very conservative views. Almost fascist. Nasty lot. It's amazing that Matea is as nice as you say she is.'

'Oh, she really is!' I could not bear any slur on the gentle girl's character. 'That's why we so want to find her – alive and happy, we hope. Luka came to the UK to bring her home here, but she really didn't want to know him. She's in love with an English boy, our neighbour's son, and they're planning to go to the USA one day, not come back here.'

The next morning, we met Lucy at the appointed time in the hotel lobby. 'A slight blip,' she informed us. 'All flights are grounded for the time being – some industrial dispute or other. But there is a good bus service to Split, takes in some lovely scenery, and I've booked you on one that sets off in half an hour, so let's go. The British Consul there will meet the bus. All laid on, you see!'

# Chapter 26

THIS WAS TURNING into a real holiday. I was enjoying the break, the change of scene, the warmer weather. I realized that ever since our move into David's house, we had met hardly anyone. Just the immediate neighbours on one side – and look at the trouble that had caused. I resolved to be more hospitable and sociable on our return. I could invite some of the people from church, for example, for a meal. Or maybe join Catherine's Gardening Club. Life would change.

Little did I know how.

Lucy delivered us to the main bus station and put on the coach to Split. There were mainly Croatian nationals on board, with just a few foreign visitors, notably a loud-voiced German couple in the seats immediately behind ours.

For nearly five hours we drove along a coastal road of breathtakingly beautiful views. As we drove along, David searched for information from his mobile phone, when he could get a signal. With mountains on one side and the Mediterranean on the other reception was patchy. He informed me about the sights as we passed, such as the magnificent cable-held Franjo Tudman Bridge and the stone wall at Ston, the longest in Europe and second in the world only to the Great Wall of China.

There was so much to admire. Islands, coves, islets, every turn in the road producing something stunning to see. I kept reminding myself that we were there really in pursuit of a missing young woman, not supposed to be enjoying ourselves.

At Neum, border guards embarked to see our passports as we were, for a few miles at least, in another country, Boznia-Herzogovina.

I dozed off for a bit when we diverted inland, but the sight of the blue Adriatic coast kept me awake for the last hour.

By early afternoon we disembarked at the waterside bus terminal in Split, and were met by a jovial red faced Croatian gentleman of middling years who shook David's hand and lifted mine to his lips. I had never had my hand kissed before, and was momentarily transported to a more gracious age. Ivo Tesla introduced himself as the Head of Mission at the UK Honorary Consulate in Split, and welcomed us effusively. As it was outside the busy tourist season, he had time to deal personally with our concerns.

He picked up and carried my small suitcase, despite it

having wheels, and beckoned us to follow him along the harbour-side to the wide, white-stoned promenade. This was obviously a major feature of the old town, and people were sauntering along between the rows of palm trees in the mild winter sunshine. Ivo pointed proudly to the high stone wall running behind much of the promenade, explaining that it had been the palace of the Roman Emperor Diocletian, and was now home to many households as well as being the cultural centre of Split.

We reached our hotel, the Marmont just off the promenade and in the centre of the picturesque old quarter. Ivo beamed as we were obviously delighted with the accommodation, and he launched into a breathless account, sounding as if he had memorised it from a tourist brochure:

'This fine hotel and the street here, the Marmontova Ulica, were named after the Napoleonic General August de Mormont who had been governor of Dalmatia in the nineteenth century and embellished Split, helping to make it the most beautiful city you see today!'

His affection for his home town was justified, based on what we had seen already. He undertook the business of our registration with the young receptionist in the small foyer, and took us to our room himself, still smiling. Before he left, he handed over a street map of Split, and marked out the address we were to visit with him the next day.

David and I wandered round the old town, finding a classy coffee shop that sold us tea. Then we sauntered through the Palace area, exploring the narrow alleys and marble-clad squares. That evening we ventured out again to find a restaurant and retired early, ready next day to meet the sinister war criminal who was our dear Matea's father.

Ivo called for us punctually at ten o'clock. He took us on foot up a broad pedestrian avenue, on pale limestone flags rubbed shiny by generations of feet, between smart shops and through colonnaded squares to where the narrow streets and alleys of the old town rise away from the harbour up the steep side of a fairly high hill. We followed our guide as he turned right and left, left and right, pausing occasionally to take our bearings and note certain landmarks as we passed.

Ivo walked quickly, used to the sharp incline and oblivious of the risk of slipping on the mirror-smooth flags. Only small chiselled incisions on the stones allowed any grip to the soles of the feet. As the slope gave way to a small area of level ground, I stopped to get my breath and to pay attention to a small grubby glazed shrine built into the wall at eye-level, with a brass icon at the back of it of the Holy Mother and Child, and a couple of dusty plastic roses placed before the image. Above the shrine was the relief carving of a skull, an inscription PMC, with a cross above the M, and the date 1712. To the left of this sad monument was the partly-defaced stone-relief of an angel. Through all the upheavals of Croatian history, world wars, civil wars and Communism, this little shrine represented the simple faith of the peasant people. Something they could hold onto to give them hope in all their troubles.

In melancholy mood, I followed the two men round the corner where they had stopped in what could hardly be called a square, just a widening of the narrow alley. Here it was not necessary to flatten ourselves against the wall when a vehicle passed, but that is all.

The men were studying the frontage of house number five, next to one where plants were growing from the cracked and partially crumbling facia-wall itself. Number five was grander than its immediate neighbours, a three-storey building with a front door positioned between two impressively grilled windows. The higher windows were shuttered and closed. David and I hung back while Ivo repeatedly rapped on a brass door knocker to alert the occupant of our presence.

Eventually the door opened, and a large broad-shouldered man emerged onto the street, coughing from the cigarette stuck onto his lower lip. His dishevelled hair was streaked with grey, but the enormous bushy moustache he sported remained defiantly black. He straightened up from a habitual stoop and growled at Ivo, who chatted amicably to him.

He coughed again, spat into the road and threw down the remnant of his cigarette, then jerked his head, inviting us into the house. I have had warmer welcomes.

We stepped into a gloomy hallway paved with black-and-white-checked tiles and followed our host into an equally dismal dining-room. Light struggled to pass through window panes thick with encrusted grime. In the centre of the room was a dark polished wooden table surrounded by six carved chairs of similar hue.

We were invited to sit on these and our host poked a newly-rolled cigarette beneath the moustache, lit it with a lighter, and coughed again. He looked at each of his visitors impassively, causing my spine to tingle. He seemed in no hurry to ask what brought us to his house. Ivo spoke in Croatian and he replied. Throughout the following conversation, Ivo translated for us, looking at David who asked the questions.

'I tell him who you are, and why you want to speak to him. I tell him you are worried about his daughter, and does not know where she is. You ask him if he know where she is. He say she has not contacted him, and he does not know where she is.'

I dreaded that reply. Then Penić/Pilić volunteered something.

'He says that he sent Luka Tušek' to bring her home, but

she tells him to go away and then she disappears.'

'Ask him where Luka is now.'

'He say he does not know. London, he thinks. Perhaps.'

'Ask him when was the last time he heard from Matea herself.'

'He says it was on the night of a party at her employers, a telephone call, but the conversation was brief because the battery of her cellphone was flat and needed to be recharged.'

'Ask if she said anything about going away, or anything that was troubling her.'

'He says no, she just say usual things. She was happy. There will be a party, but first she will go to somewhere for a meal with friends.'

There followed a monologue from Matea's father, of which Ivo relayed the gist. David's look at me carried all the disappointment that I was feeling too.

Mr Pilić he says that Matea had become a different girl. Not the obedient one she had been. She refused Luka, which very much upset Mr Pilić. He says Luka is a good young man for her, but he is afraid she will not be a good wife. Too independent now. Maybe not even a virgin. He wants her to return at once to him here in Split.'

'We'd love to tell her to do that,' I blurted.

'Ask him why he moved here from Dubrovnik?' I felt David was treading on thin ice with that one.

I was not wrong. On hearing the question in his own language, the man's swarthy face reddened even more and he shouted something, scraped back his chair, and gestured to the door. When Ivo said something placatory, he sat again and muttered something reluctantly.

Ivo explained, saying that Matea had told him that she had

received threatening letters saying that someone, probably a Serb, knew who he really was and what he had done. That frighten him very much, so he is leaving his town.'

That made sense. With no further questions, we thanked the old war criminal and the three of us left, relieved to be in the fresh air and bright sunshine. Ivo was smiling, sure that he had performed a great service.

The journey home was miserable. Although we had a better sense of where Matea came from, and with what she had to put up, we were no further forward in finding her.

# Chapter 27

THEN IT HAPPENED.

News about Matea.

It was on a day shortly after our return from Croatia. I was left to take care of the elder Deanes while Helena took herself by bus to the community theatre, the Roses, in the small but busy medieval town of Tewkesbury. The bus-stop could not have been more convenient, just outside the house and alongside the telephone box, now housing a public access defibrillator, at the end of the drive. My mother was only in her midfifties but enjoyed the morning film screenings for 'seniors', with free coffee refills and ready companionship. Her routine involved wandering round the shops after the screening, or strolling beside the river, with or without just-made acquaintances. I did not expect her back until late afternoon.

After she left I called round to the Fletchers to see how James was shaping. He had been discharged from hospital after only a couple of days and was spending time at home recuperating. While resting, he was able to keep up his studies online, but was wanting some light reading to give relief. Just before flying off to Dubrovnik I had introduced him to P.G. Wodehouse and was now feeding his new addiction by lending him our Jeeves books one by one. I took with me *Stiff Upper Lip, Jeeves*, and it was gratefully received. He was looking pale, and concern for Matea was holding back his recovery. As ever, I spoke the usual platitudes of 'I'm sure she'll be all right. You're not to worry. Just get better yourself.'

I returned to a few hours of my own reading. I felt I was making fairly good progress with the book considering all the dramas and worries of recent weeks. The biographical sections were almost compete on Fanny Burney's two brothers, James, an explorer, and Charles Jr., a classics scholar who donated his massive book and newspaper collection to the British Library; her beloved sister Suzanna Elizabeth Phillips, and her half-sister and novelist, Sarah Harriet Burney. Other family members including her father Dr Charles and mother Elizabeth Sleep, the stepmother, and various talented cousins, plus Fanny herself, still needed working on. Mainly that involved cutting down rather than building up, but that itself required lots of effort if all the salient and interesting points are kept and only the dull or unimportant ones glanced over or ignored.

I prepared a parsnip soup and sandwich lunch for three and took it upstairs, where I shared it with the senior Deanes. Anthony was more sleepy than usual and had to be constantly cajoled into swallowing his soup, and Terri was more on edge as a result. I don't know which was the more trying and wished Helena were home to deal with this. I was never cut out to be a nurse.

Lunch over, I brought the used crockery on a tray down the stairs and into the kitchen. I was just running the water to wash them when the main outside door opened. I called out 'Helena?' and held my breath as she did not reply. Instead the kitchen door opened and in walked a very serious-faced David.

'Julia, I'm afraid I've some really bad news to bring you. There're some colleagues in a car outside, so I can't be long now.'

I drew out a chair and sat down. I had to, as my knees were buckling. I guessed.

'I had to come to tell you first, before I go to the Fletchers. I do hope Melissa's not there, they'll need to prepare how they're going to tell her.'

'Go on. It's about Matea, isn't it?'

'Well, the body of a young woman has been found, rather decomposed. It's been a mild winter, hasn't it? It was pulled from a culvert next to the Avon this morning, over in Worcestershire, and we reckon, well, we're sure, it's Matea.'

'Oh God! Oh God, no!' I wailed and held my face in my hands. They were trembling. I was soon shaking all over, and sobbing, and denying its possibility, while knowing the news was sure.

David drew up another chair and sat close, putting his arm around my shoulder, then rose to fetch the box of tissues I kept next to the radio on the dresser. I snuffled and sniffed and gasped, barely able to comprehend the finality of that announcement. Dead. After all that, dead. And nearby, relatively. Not in Split nor Dubrovnik, but here in the West of England. Too awful and too sad.

'I know, love. I know what she meant to you. I'm cut up too, and I know mum and dad will be, and I dread to think of Melissa. Well look, it would be good if you made yourself a cup of tea now. I've got to go to break it to Catherine and James. It won't be easy. God, after all they've gone through, and now this. I'll be back soon as.'

The tea was tasteless, the addition of salt tears not helping. David returned within half an hour, during which time I had done nothing but blub. As he entered, I resolved to pull myself together, and asked how the Fletchers had taken the news.

'Well... Catherine's gone to identify the body. She took it fairly well, saying that she expected as much after all this time. I'm afraid that James was shaken badly. He screamed "No, no!" and burst into tears. I couldn't stay, he was too distraught. I guess he needs time to get over it. Fortunately he did not ask for details...'

This sounded ominous. I had wondered, but had not liked to ask. David however braced himself and told me.

'As I said, decomposition had set in, but it seems there might have been a sexual assault of some kind. She was wearing no trousers, or pants, or those boots ... Just a red blouse, no bra... There could be an element of robbery too as her handbag was not there either. Anyway, we're keeping all options open until we get more information and the PM results. I really cannot say more – probably said too much already. Please don't tell anyone else in the house any of those details – just that she's dead, probably drowned. I don't want the papers knowing'

I continued just to sit there, and allowed myself to be gently led onto my feet and out of the kitchen into our sitting room. There, on one of our large soft easy chairs I succumbed again to another bout of uncontrollable tears and sobbing while I could hear David back in the kitchen clinking some ice into a couple of tumblers. He appeared with them, took a bottle out of our drinks cupboard and splashed some Scotch into the glasses. He handed me one. Just then Terri appeared having followed him from the kitchen, and just stood silently watching, grim-faced.

'So, I take it she's dead then?' she said quietly. I imagined from the way she looked at me that she was uncomfortable with my display of emotion. She slowly turned away and David presented her with the tumbler he had brought for himself. He went back to get another glass while Terri perched on one of the upright chairs and sipped without saying a further word. No tears, no sobs, just a series of deep breaths. I felt a surge of anger towards her. Did she not feel anything? Was she heroically mastering her emotions, or did she just not have any? Why do such cold-fish people look as if they think themselves superior to people who express their feelings? I stopped myself in time from saying something spiteful out loud and felt a twinge of self-righteousness in the mastery of my baser feeling. I needed at that moment someone to cling to, a soft warm body to hug. Helena! I suddenly missed Helena and hoped she would be home soon so that I could weep on her shoulder.

David was doing his best, but something was missing. I had been thinking these thoughts for a while, but was now firmly convinced. The lack of warmth, the distancing of the formerly loving, sensitive, tactile, David that he had been before. In our London days. The David I once knew had changed. I couldn't put my finger on it, but something must have happened, or was happening, and I didn't like it. I was not comfortable. He was leaving me out of somewhere deep within him. He and I were no longer one body, one soul, one item – there, I've said it. We were just two people who happened to live together and were going through a bad time. Constant responsibility for ageing parents was not helping. The senior Deanes are not even really old, just frail with ill-health and poor physiques. There could be years ahead, with David disappearing like the Cheshire cat, leaving only his breathing empty body behind.

I was wallowing, caught up in my own world. Then I felt worse because of the guilt of self-pity, when the loss of Matea's young life was what I should be bewailing. I stood up, downed my whisky, and went upstairs to relay such details as necessary to Tony.

He was visibly upset. Poor thing. His life was confined to his room, being tended to now only by one misery-soaked wife and my scatty mother. He was a man of quiet dignity and intelligence, and had been highly esteemed by the community, as town councillor and patron of several local charities. When I had first known him he was at the height of his powers, head of his law firm, chairman of the Tewkesbury Conservative Association and the recipient of an MBE. In happier times, he and Terri would spend Christmases with us in London, and he was invariably good company at table and on rambles over Hampstead Heath.

Terri's company, on the other hand, I tolerated but could not enjoy. If there was a negative comment that could be made, she would make it. Praise was just the absence of criticism. She knew how to 'suck the joy' out of life, as Marge Simpson probably said. How did David bear to grow up in such a household? How could he have turned out as he did, in his better moments – good-natured, optimistic, even humorous? All my musings those days, all my waking hours when I was not working, tended to turn towards David and our relationship.

# Chapter 28

MY LIFE WENT ON – diminished now in knowing I would never again see and speak with Matea, never hear her laugh or rely on her quiet caring of my parents-in-law. For weeks I felt an element of 'survivors guilt' when any small pleasure, any little enjoyment, felt like a betrayal, an act of uncaring. Even the earliest signs of Spring failed to rally me.

I would find myself imagining how that war-criminal of her father reacted when he heard the news. Would it hit him that his grief was the same that was felt by those whose relatives and friends had met their deaths by his hands? Did it lead him to feel remorse? Or was anger and a thirst for revenge overwhelming him – as it did me, too, at times? Who could do that to a sweet young girl?

Was Matea yet another victim of the Balkan Wars of the 1990s? Was her killer motivated in the same way as James's attacker had been, but from another conflict?

Was O'Neill not really the killer of Ian Fletcher, as he protested, and whoever it was had come back to take out the only witness to the shooting?

Then again, what had she been witness to in the farm shed the time we followed Konstantinou? Was our road accident, being driven off the road, connected with that and with her death?

Or was she the prey simply of a vicious sexual predator who happened upon her as she strode out of the Fletcher's house after an argument?

The more I thought about it, the more frustrated I felt. Couldn't the police, yes including David, work harder and deeper and come up with the answers?

I felt more alone than I had ever done. I could not get into David's mind any more and he did not seem to want to read mine. We were leading lives in parallel, but separately. My grief over Matea was something I was left alone to feel, without him.

David was working harder and longer hours than ever he had done in London. I could tell that he was frustrated at not being the lead investigator into Matea's murder, as it was thought he was too close to the victim. Another member of the Brunel team was leading the trawl through every scrap of evidence and the questioning of every suspect and witness. The lengthy time between the Matea's death and the discovery of her body made the job of finding the perpetrator so much more difficult.

David was involved still in the cases of the Fletcher murder and the assault on James. Although evidence was plentiful, the two suspects, O'Neill and Williams, had withdrawn their confessions and were threatening to plead Not Guilty even to wounding James. It seems they believed that having their say in court was worth the probable conviction for murder and consequent mandatory life sentences. There was still a lot of paperwork and standard police procedure before the two could face a jury. Evidence on the murder charge was wanting, especially without the only eye-witness. These were the reasons David gave for now spending almost every evening at work, sometimes not returning until past midnight.

One night, at about nine o'clock, I was reading in the sitting room, legs pulled up under me, a mug of decaf on the coffee table, and a CD of Haydn quartets quietly playing. Of a sudden I heard a muffled thump and a cry from the room above mine, and raced up the back stairs to find Tony sitting on the floor beside his bed. Terri was just standing, rubbing her hands together with anxiety, but Helena was bending over him asking if anything hurt.

'No, no. I'm fine,' he said. 'Just a little bruised, maybe. Nothing too painful. No hips or anything. Can you give me a lift up?'

My mother and I then helped him up, supporting his back until he was sitting on the bed. We then swung his legs carefully until he was lying in his usual position, propped up on pillows. His apologies were unnecessary and, frankly, embarrassing. He had misjudged the distance to the edge of the bed after using his commode, and had fallen, fortunately rather slowly.

I left Helena pouring water for Tony to take some sedatives for shock, and returned to my sitting room. At once I telephoned David's desk at Prism House, to let him know what had happened. The weary voice that answered denied that David was there, saying that he had left many hours before, 'He said he was going home. Sorry, can't help.'

Funny.

Hours passed.

'Where were you, at about nine o'clock tonight?' I tried to keep my tone light. But something of edge must have come through.

'Why? Working, of course. Where I've been every night.'

I told him about his father and why I needed to contact him.

'Why not use my mobile?' His tone was accusatory. 'I've told you before, don't ring me at work. Use my mobile, if you have to.'

He went up to see his father and returned, satisfied that all was well upstairs and everyone sleeping peacefully. It was true that he had told me not to ring him at work. I don't know why I hadn't – too flustered about his father, probably.

But it rankled. Why could I not speak to him wherever he was?

# Chapter 29

ONE SUNNY AFTERNOON in March I fulfilled the invitation I had received to visit a fellow member of the Burney Society, an organization of enthusiasts I had joined on leaving Queen's. This member lived in the nearest large village to Tredington, Bishops Cleeve. She had been insisting for weeks that we should meet, but, with one thing and another...

We spent a pleasant couple of hours drinking tea and discussing members of the Burney family and their friends and acquaintances as if they had been personally known to us. We found plenty to laugh about, and I was offered the loan of an out-of-print book from her that I had long been seeking.

As it was a fine, sunny afternoon, and still light, we went for a walk through the village to the parish church. This magnificent structure, dating from the twelfth century, is one of those rare ones for which the local Anglicans and Roman Catholics had legally arranged to share, and it formed part of the cluster of parishes served by the priest I knew at Tewkesbury. We admired the traces of medieval wall paintings and the oldest oak staircase in England, used by bell ringers to access the tower. After pausing at the recumbent effigies of the seventeenth-century notables, Richard de la Bere and his wife, my new friend led me up a narrow winding staircase at the west end of the church to an old school room, which houses the display of a collection of old village photographs and memorabilia. A painted, or stencilled, fierce tiger decorates one wall, an educational visual aid from the early Victorian era.

We strolled back to her house, and parted, promising exchanges of Burney-focused information either here at her house or at mine.

I collected my car from her drive and was intending to leave Bishop's Cleeve when I decided to do some shopping in the Tesco supermarket  there. I was always in need of bread and ingredients for easy vegetarian meals, as Helena's repertoire was rather limited.

I drove around looking for a parking space, trawling along each section and beginning to despair of ever finding one, when I spotted  a gap between a small white van and a bright red Mazda. As I reversed into the space I noticed the vehicle parked behind mine was a large black Landrover  SUV.

I felt a sudden shiver.

Intent on discovering more, I got out and walked towards the back of my car and then, in the narrow space between the back of mine and front of the SUV, I  crossed in front of it, intent on inspecting the passenger side for evidence of having rammed the Rover, several months before. As I expected, there was a small dent on the passenger side of the front panel and a larger one on the front curb.

I felt an adrenaline rush and a sudden pounding in my chest. I took my phone from my shoulder bag and took photographs of the damaged metalwork. Then I stepped round to the rear of the vehicle and, with a sickening lump that suddenly stuck in my throat, saw what was boldly displayed on the wheel-cover attached to the back of the SUV – a snarling tiger's head. My second tiger within an hour! I took a step backwards to get the image in camera view and raised it to take in the shot.

'Fuck you, bitch!'

This greeting came from behind me, the charming unseen speaker rapidly closing in so that he was almost knocking me over. I could feel him and smell him.

'Get in, now! Get in the bloody car.'

With his body pressing me forward, I was propelled along the side of the SUV, silent and unresistant with shock. He reached forward over my shoulder with his left arm, grabbed the handle of the passenger door and flung it open, his bulk behind me preventing any escape. Another character climbed into the driver's side as my abductor pushed me upwards and into the passenger seat and continued pushing until I shuffled along towards the driver. The charmer behind me climbed in and sat alongside, sandwiching me between his bulk and the skinnier body of the driver.

I turned to catch a view of the man to my left, but was first assailed by the stench of his breath, a pungent mixture of beer, curry and tobacco. A late lunch, no doubt. His ruddy, unshaven face, in contrast to his colleague's gaunt pale one, bore a snarling grimace that chilled my already shivering body. As the driver reversed out of his space and drove towards the car park exit, the brute on my left growled,

'Gimme the phone, NOW!'

I didn't argue, but handed it over meekly, mewling pathetically. I would have made a totally useless agent in Gestapo hands. What a wimp. I embarrass myself just thinking about it.

We turned left out of the car park, heading towards the

racecourse, and thence Cheltenham. My seat-mate withdrew a phone of his own from his back jeans pocket, an operation that came near to groping me, and made a call. As we were held up at the bypass roundabout, his voice and the answering one came over clearly,

'Mr K,' he addressed his interlocutor, 'we've got a situation. A bad one'

'Watcha mean? Whatcha done now?'

'We've picked up dat bitch, v'one we drove off of v' road. V' one wiv de nosey bitch in. Y'know? Vis is t'driver, assa what I'm sayin', innit? She wiz takin' photos of de car, round de back, and de number. Whatcha want us to do wiv her, K?'

I could hear a minor explosion at the other end.

'You fucking twats! You wanna good smack, the both of you! What ya done to 'er?'

'Nuffink, K. We ain't done nuffink to 'er. Yet. We gotta phone, is all. She's 'ere in d' car, in't she. D'ya want 'er doing?'

'No, you pillocks, I don't want her doing! Whatcha think? Where are you? Where were you when you got her?'

'Tesco car park, Mr K, Bishop's Cleeve. We're comin' uppa d' rugby club.' We slowed down towards a set of lights at red, then sped through even before the green was lit.

'You know what supermarket car parks have, you pair of muffin-brains? Cameras, that's what! The sort that check who'sa coming in, who'sa going out. You're right on bloody candid camera, you dick-heads.'

I admired his range of insulting epithets, and the way they were obviously disconcerting his henchmen.

'Get her out RIGHT NOW!' barked the delightful man, my saviour. But he added, 'And destroy her phone, the SIM card especially. And you'll have to dump the car now – idiots.'

.

176

I could not tell what his accent was, but made a guess that it was Greek, and that Mr K was none other than Konstantinou. I couldn't wait to tell David, but without my phone that would have to wait. The two accomplices, by their own admission, were those who had nearly killed us some months before.

They drove into the racecourse 'park and ride' car park, to the area furthest from the road. Fatty got out and dragged me after him by my arm. He had no need to pull as I was more than willing to escape. Leaving me on the outside, feeling almost ecstatic with relief, I watched him climb back in and the oversized car sped away while I tried to catch sight of, and remember, the number plate. VX13 U.., or something like that. Just at that moment a green D bus heading to Bishops Cleeve was pulling in and I sped across the car park and caught it just in time. I got out at the village and soon was flopping into the driver's seat of my car.

Only then did my body go into reaction mode, and I wept and shook and sobbed out loud, to the consternation of the owners of the red Mazda I had parked alongside. A middle-aged woman wearing a beanie hat and a worried frown, tapped on my window and asked if I was all right.

I nodded tearfully at her, and thanked her for her concern. Despite the shakes, and the nausea that suddenly hit me, I managed to drive safely the few miles home.

I had half believed, romantic fool that I am, that David, on hearing of my ordeal, would wrap his arms around me and mutter consoling words, such as 'Oh my Darling. You're safe. That's all that matters.'

No, life is not like that.

After the explosion of anger and shouted accusations at me that I had, once again and against all common sense, put myself in harm's way, David simply walked out, got back into his car, and drove off.

I sat in the kitchen, utterly deflated, upset and angry with my spouse for his lack of support. The door opened and Helena put her head round it hesitantly.

'Can I come in?'

'Of course. I've just had a really bad experience and David has just walked out. Not even a hug!'

That opened the floodgates, and when I came to I was surprised to find myself standing up and held in the arms of my mother. This must have been a first.

'How are things between you?' she asked, looking more tender than just curious.

I told her about the lack of warmth in our relationship. I even mentioned our lack of bedroom activity, contrasting it with the healthily robust sex-life we had led in London.

'I know he finds it hard, here, with his parents in the same house. But I feel it's not just that. Is it me? Am I so different?'

'No, love. You're just the same. Still kind and funny, just like you always were.'

Taken aback by this unexpected praise I saw she was still looking at me almost pityingly.

'Do you think David could have changed?' she asked. I looked blank. 'Maybe he's finding his new job too much, under too much stress.'

'Hardly!' I retorted. 'The Met was stressful. There were murders almost every week for him there. But he does seem to be working harder, or longer hours anyway.'

She still had that look. As if she knew something.

'Listen, mother, Helena, if you know something I don't, tell me, for God's sake.' I was almost shouting.

She looked down, deep in thought. Then slowly turned

her face towards mine, and spoke, almost in a whisper, words I never thought to hear.

'Look, Petal. It may be nothing, really nothing. But..'

'BUT?'

'But, all right. One night, a few months ago now, after I got back from Bournemouth, I must have caught a chill as I woke in the night with a sore throat and had this dreadful urge to have a drop of whisky, or brandy or something, to relieve it. I knew David and you kept a bottle in your sitting room, so I came downstairs and was just about to open the door fully and turn on the light when I heard David was there, talking on his mobile, in the dark. I stood in the doorway, with the door ajar, and ...'

'And? What was he saying? Hey, how could you eavesdrop like that?'

'Never mind that now. He was talking to someone he was calling 'Darling', and I knew it wasn't you – you were in bed, asleep I expect. He was telling this person that he couldn't see them for a few days as he was going away, Croatia I think he said...'

She carried on talking, but I heard not a word.

# Chapter 30

AFTER DAVID TOLD me that he had arrested Konstantinou and was detaining him while a thorough investigation took place, I told him my news.

'I'm going back to London.'

'What? What d'you mean? How long for?'

'Ever, maybe.'

I told him that I had arranged to move back into our old Camden flat as Louisa had split up with her boyfriend and would be glad of the help in paying the rent. My book was at a critical

.

stage of completion and I could do without the distractions of the rogues and villains of Gloucestershire that were blighting my life.

'Besides,' I added with what I hoped would seem stiletto-like precision, 'you won't miss me. You'll be able to see more of your beloved Darling, and she can look after your bloody parents. I haven't asked Helena if she wants to stay when I've gone. It's up to her.'

David left, without a word, without a denial and without the slightest attempt to dissuade me.

The next time David addressed me, sitting beside me at the kitchen table, the only space I cared to share with him, was with his own momentous news.

Konstantinou had been charged with people trafficking and multiple cases of child abuse. Apparently the sight that had so terrified Matea that day when we had been driven off the road was of a row of naked children and young women being examined, like cattle at a market, by prospective buyers from all over the UK.

By using the farm building, all physical traces were able to be obliterated by herding real animals into the space. The gang had fled the scene, and their victims been removed by lorry, as soon as Matea had been spotted looking in through the window.

Konstantinou's agency, providing legitimate nurses and au pairs from Eastern Europe, was the perfect cover for his illegal enterprise. Had it not been for my short-lived abduction from the Tesco car park, the police would not have been able to gain the necessary proof of Konstantinou's involvement. The traffic cops had run down the SUV just south of Cheltenham, before the fat charmer and the ghoul had had time to dispose of it. The two miscreants had willingly fingered their boss rather than take on themselves the credit for their activities.

I felt elated. My little escapade had led to a good result.

Ha! How many innocent victims would now be spared

this inhumane, this most vile of crimes.

'Well, that's one mystery solved – what Matea had seen. No wonder she was so shocked she could not remember it. What a sight. Now, what about the other, the Fletcher murder? Any further on with that?'

'Quite far, actually. The two clowns, O'Neill and Williams, keep changing their pleas as we find out more and more. Now they are going for guilty on the wounding James and manslaughter on the Ian Fletcher shooting. Apparently they only meant to hurt him, as they did James, according to them. It seems there was nobody else involved. Just as we thought.'

I accepted that news now with equilibrium. David's obvious satisfaction with the result of his work did not move me. The fact that he had kept the developments from me until I asked only reinforced my lack of caring about his success. At one time I would have been jubilant and celebrated with fizz, smiles and hugs. Now I was just numb.

David, whose sleeping arrangements now involved the long sofa in the sitting room, must have sensed my mood. He tried a form of reconciliation. He moved his hand towards mine, attempting to cover it with his.

Not going to happen. I removed mine sharply away and continued sorting out papers on the table.

'I'm sorry, David. It'll take more than that. Until you convince me that you are not seeing anyone, anyone at all, I'm off. I'm moving my things into the flat at the beginning of April, when teaching finishes. I need Louisa there to help me move in.'

David looked hangdog, more miserable than I had seen him look. Distraught even.

'Ever since we've moved out here, everything has fallen apart. My whole world has gone West, literally.'

.

'I know. I'm sorry,' he said lamely. 'Let me sort it out. I didn't mean to do this to you, honestly. It happened so gradually, from when you were still in London and I was here alone during the week. She, I won't say who, was good company. At first, that all it was. Just a colleague helping me to settle in, being friendly. I'll break it off, I promise. I'll try to make it up to you, but I can see that you need some time on your own. I respect that. But please,' he as almost choking with tears. 'Don't consider anything as final. This isn't the end – it can't be. We mean too much to each other.'

I looked at my David, my first love, my life. And I felt no pity. I felt nothing.

'Let's see,' I said.

# Chapter 31

AT THE BEGINNING of April, towards one o'clock, David telephoned from police headquarters. I took the call upstairs in Tony's bed-sitting room.

'Put your television on. Get the news. You'll be interested, I know.'

I was indeed when I heard and saw the news headlines on the lunchtime bulletin:

.

## MATEA – SERBIAN YOUTH ARRESTED ON
## SUSPICION OF MURDER

There were photographs of both Zivko and Matea, and a map of the Balkans, showing the two countries. Everyone in the country must have known who Matea was from all the earlier media coverage. The newscaster was reminding people of the war between the elements of the former Yugoslavia twentyfive or so years before.

I was eating with Tony and Terri, who had gone very quiet while that item was on. It was their habit to watch the news over lunch, Tony from his bed eating from a tray, and Terri and I at the small table, both facing the screen. I cleared up, took the dirty dishes down to the kitchen, and went back to work. The book was progressing well and was almost at the proofreading stage. Then the telephone rang.

It was Catherine asking me to go round for a cup of tea and a chat. 'It's something rather urgent.' She added, 'Just you. Can you not bring your mother with you.'

That was no problem. 'She went earlier to collect Melissa. There were things Melissa needs to bring home before the holidays. Including a cake she has baked.'

I lost no time in getting round to the Fletchers' kitchen, where Catherine was ready with a teapot and already pouring into delicate china cups. I was all interest, and sat as directed at the table.

'James is out with the dogs. That's why it's so quiet in here. Well, this is difficult for me,' she began, and twitched her mouth in the way I had seen James doing when nervous. She sat and after pouring, handed me my cup. Finally she broke the silence.

'I saw they had arrested that Serbian lad this morning.

David did that, did he?'

'No, DCI King, his colleague on the Zephyr team, you know, the serious crime unit.'

'Well, I know you have linked those nasty notes Matea received with the person who killed her. But there really isn't a link.'

Now my skin began to develop goosebumps. 'How do you know?'

'Well, you'll probably find out sooner or later. That was me. Not killed her, you understand. Just wrote those notes. Just wait here a moment.'

While I was digesting this bombshell, and my head swirling with questions, she returned with something wrapped up in cloth.

'I keep this locked in the gun room. Not in the cabinets, but in a drawer, with the key hidden from prying eyes. Look at it.'

She unwrapped an old-fashioned revolver with a six-inch barrel. I blanched.

'Don't worry, although it is loaded, ever since that Irishman came here and shot Ian. Makes me feel a bit safer, knowing that I could protect myself. But this is a remarkable firearm.'

'I don't get the connection…'

'This was a personal gift from Marshal Tito to my father.'

I felt excited and confused in equal measure, and just kept switching my stare between the gun and Catherine, waiting for her to tell the story she was obviously aching to do.

'My father was a hero of the SOE during the second world war. Wonderful man. Not a nerve in his body. He was sent to help our allies, the Yugoslav partisans, working alongside Brigadier, later Sir, Fitzroy Maclean. He helped to supply the partisans with arms and gave and gathered information against the Nazis. Tito was so close to him – at some points they even fought side by side – that he gave him this, his own revolver, as a souvenir, and invited him to visit after the war. He did. We went as a family several times when I was a child, and frequently stayed with the Macleans in their Croatian home. I'm good with languages and picked up Serbo-Croat, as we called it then, pretty quickly. Then I went on to study it at university. It's different, you know, from the usual Mediterranean ones.'

'That's how you could write the notes!'

'Of course. I'm fluent, though I never let on to Matea. She needed to speak English, and I wasn't going to give her an easy way out. Plus it was useful to know what she said about me when she spoke on the phone to her father. I knew about the father. I had been on the Balkan desk as a Croatia specialist in GCHQ during the 90s, listening in to telephone and clandestine field-radio conversations.'

'But you said your job was a lowly one, a dull one?'

'Well, we are not meant to talk about what we do there, and it is easier to avoid that if I suggest it was some dull clerical work. Actually, it can be very dull, waiting up all night in the chance someone will communicate telephonically with some else of importance. Anyway, I was inspired, if that's what you can call it, by that odious Irishman, the one that shot Ian; raking up old wars and disputes. So I decided to embellish the young Serb's grudge against Croatians in the hope of scaring Matea off for good.'

'Off what?'

'Off staying here – off getting fixed up with James. I need him here, with me.'

She softened her tone, 'He is so good with Melissa, and now Ian is not here, the place needs a man about it. There are plenty of good jobs waiting for him in the area. I know of several firms that are crying out for people with his expertise. He must stay here, not go running off with the first foreign girl who happens to catch his eye. Oh, I know she was nice enough. But she wouldn't have stayed for good. Not here, right here. There was even talk of them going to America. Well, really! They thought I didn't know, but I did. I won't tell you how.'

'Why didn't you just ask her to leave?'

'Ah, you're joking. For one thing, we had a contract, and I sure as hell was not the one going to break it. It had to come from her. Anyway, James was not to know I was involved or he'd have been furious; might even have driven him away altogether. He'd never have forgiven me. He'd have joined her, wherever she was and probably not have spoken to me ever again!'

'So you're saying you did this, but not...'

'Kill? Oh no, of course not. There's a world of difference. I just couldn't have you thinking it was that Serbian boy. Anyway, you would have found out eventually I'm sure, what with all that DNA testing and such like. I'm surprised you hadn't done it already.

Now you've got to go after the person who really killed her. My money is on that Luka from Dubrovnik. The language he used about her – of course, he did not know I could understand – but it showed the violence he felt towards her. I've always thought it could be him – or the Russian lad, Piotr, although it seems he'd been off the scene for a while before Matea was killed.'

'Or', I added, 'personally, I think it's Konstantinou. After all he nearly killed her once before. It's just, I don't know. He didn't hurt me when he could have, when his thugs kidnapped me.'

'Well, that leaves my other theory – that someone, some stranger, took advantage of her as she was walking along, raped

.

and killed her then dumped her body in that culvert.'

'Possibly. But the tragic thing is that, if she'd been left on dry land, she'd be OK. She drowned...'

'No!' screeched Catherine, dropping her cup onto the table, missing the saucer. 'No! She was dead already!....Ah!'

My eyes could not have widened further. I'm sure my mouth dropped open. Certainly we both froze. I sat like a statue made of ice.

'Ah,' I repeated, lamely.

'Bugger!' She quickly composed herself. 'I mean, I understood ... The reports said...she had been dead first, before going into the water.'

My look had not changed. I thought a hundred useless thoughts in quick succession, mainly of the futility of fight or flight with that loaded gun just feet away.

She followed my look down at the table. Her body seemed to slump; all fight gone.

'All right. Now you know. Good heavens!. It wasn't meant to go that way. I called you here to prevent you looking at me as a suspect for the murder. Oh well. Shame about this.'

She folded her hand over the gun. Suddenly I was all composure. Keep her talking, was the phrase that came to me. Melissa will be home soon. I'll escape then. So long as we talk, I'm alive.

'Why?' Ridiculous question. 'Why did you do it? I'm sure you didn't mean to.'

'Why? I'll tell you why! No, of course I didn't mean to kill her, or even harm her. Not really. But, well, that silly cow wasn't put off by the notes, was she? She and James became even closer. He would have left  for America with her. For good! So I had to do something. I had the perfect plan.'

'Tell me!' The longer it takes, the better. Amazing how

clear-headed I could be in this situation, although I was sure she could hear my heart pounding.

'Well, unless she decided that James wasn't the one for her, wasn't the right man, Matea would keep her claws in him and he would do whatever she wanted. So, I decided I'd get her to think he had been less than a gentleman.'

She looked triumphant as she spoke, but I was further perplexed.

'One of the main reasons she told me she liked James. Liked!' she broke off to snort derisorily. She continued, 'She liked him because he never tried to take advantage of her. He "respected" her.'

She positively spat out that word as if it had been toxic.

She continued, 'So, the idea of a wild party came to me. A party where all sorts of things would go on. Things that would explode that notion she had of James the Gentleman. I know enough of what goes on during parties of young people – see enough of the aftermath before me in court!'

'I don't see how you could have been sure things would have turned out that way with these kids. They seemed a nice, respectable bunch of young people.'

'Aha! They might have been, but what do you think I put in the punch? It wasn't just an ordinary hangover those kids suffered from, with the ordinary alcohol-induced amnesia. No, I used Rohypnol. The old sort, before they started putting a sort of dye in it to detect it. On the bench I'd come across cases of date-rape using the stuff, so got hold of some. You know the drug started out as a legitimate sleeping aid, very effective, and that's what I wanted it for. It wasn't difficult with a private prescription some years back, and Ian would use it in small doses to help him sleep. The pain of his cancer was sometimes unbearable and without that drug I don't know how he would ever have slept. And if he didn't, I couldn't. Anyway, mixed with alcohol it's tasteless and powerful. It put the whole crowd of those friends of James into a deep sleep almost at once.'

'And the row? The one between Matea and James that you say you heard?'

'There was no row. I made that up! When they were all unconscious, I rolled Matea over closer to James. She was so light. I took off her clothes and boots and was about to make it look as though he had tried to have his way with her.'

'Gosh, could you do that? Wasn't it difficult?'

'Not at all. They all slept so soundly, every single one of them. The hope was that when she woke up, she'd have been furious with him. Taking advantage of her, practically rape. There'd have been a terminal row, that sort of thing. You know how she made a big virtue of her precious virginity. Old fashioned, these Croatians, even now, and although they may not be as Catholic as they once were.'

'What happened? What went wrong?'

Keep it going, at all costs. Question everything. Delay, delay.

'Well, as I was rolling her along the floor, I realised that Matea was not just unconscious. She was actually dead. That's why she couldn't have drowned! She was dead already.'

She was speaking now more rapidly, in a tone of rising desperation. 'The accident and the medication from the hospital must have reacted with the Rohypnol. I really never intended that. I had not thought it possible. Dead!'

'So what did you do?' I resisted the urge to ask why she had not called 999 and tried to seek help. Maybe poor Matea could have been revived. After all, I knew she was not dead at that stage.

'Well, I panicked rather, naturally. Think of the scandal!

I'd have lost everything – being a JP, James, everything… So, I put that shirt on her again, but chucked her clothes and boots, oh, and handbag, into a black plastic sack and carried it, and then her, outside – she was not much heavier than one of my Labradors, and I've lugged them around before now, in the vets for instance. So I got her into James' car, one she'd been in many times before, so no surprise to find her DNA there. I wore gloves, of course. Not stupid. I went upstairs and grabbed her passport and money, couldn't see her mobile, didn't really think about it as I knew the batteries had been flat and she'd lost the charger earlier that day. Then I took her navy jacket, stuffed it into the plastic sack, and drove around.'

'Did you know where you were going?'

'Not really at first. I knew two things – I had to avoid passing those number plate recognition cameras. Fortunately I'd worked out where they were around here from police evidence at several trials I'd heard. There are not too many, especially on minor country roads. They cost thousands, you know? Then it had to be water, to wash off any clues, and I thought it better to go into another police area, Worcestershire, so as to delay identification, and so on.'

'You could think so clearly?'

'You can when your back is against the wall!'

I added to myself, 'Like my position, right now!'

She continued, 'I remembered this place near Evesham, Fladbury, close to where I was brought up. There the road crosses the Avon at the tiny Jubilee Bridge, and there's a little ditch, a sort of small tributary, running into the river right by the road and covered in brambles and undergrowth. I found it, even in the dark. It's pretty deserted round there at the best of times. And this was about midnight, remember. She was dead, I swear it. Not breathing and as pale as a ghost. I just opened the car door, dragged her out – even as a deadweight she was really very light – and chucked her into the culvert. I had to push her right down, below the brambles. She was well hidden.'

'You didn't hold her down, under the water?'

'Didn't need to, she was face down anyway. And dead already, I told you!'

'Then what?' I was desperate to keep her talking.

'On the way home I found some wheelie bins waiting to be emptied, a whole row of them outside some cottages in Cropthorne, and took the  plastic sack with her clothes and passport and stuffed it down under household rubbish. No-one looks in these bins before the machinery scrunches them up, so I knew they wouldn't be found. By the time I got back,  all was quiet, apart from some snoring coming from the sitting room.'

'The perfect murder!'

'Except it wasn't murder. I'm telling you. It was manslaughter at most. The medicines combined with the drug and drink. That's what did it! I didn't want her to die, just be furious with James and walk out of his life and mine  forever.'

'Well, OK. Sounds reasonable.' I said it, but didn't mean it. I thought it the worst thing I had heard. Life behind bars, for ever, would be too good for her. After all that agony of not knowing, week after week, and she knew everything all the time.

'Perhaps if you just repeated what you just told me to David; explained to him..'

'Not going to happen, darling. Not for a moment. They'll wonder where you got to, but you'll not be able to tell anyone anything pretty soon.'

She gripped the revolver firmly and pointed the end of the barrel towards me. Why did I mention David?

'On your feet, Julia. I'm sorry to have to do this, but you

give me no choice. Go on, out of the house.'

I did not argue, as I was suddenly engaged, mentally and physically, with trying not to wet my pants. Fear is no friend of dignity. I went through the gunroom and out at the side door, and she was soon just behind me, shutting the door behind her. We turned  left towards the garden and walked on. I tried walking as slowly as I could without upsetting her, playing for every last second of time.  Just as we passed a wooden shed, she told me to stop, to step into it and to pick up the spade that was just inside.

'Don't even think of doing anything with it, other than carry it. Go on, towards the gate into the lane.'

I did as bidden  and we carried on in this odd Indian-file trek over the lawn, taking the direct route to the gate. I arrived first, wondering desperately if I could slam it shut and run along the lane into my garden before she caught up with me. But it was a gun she held, and the  momentary advantage would be ruined by one well-aimed shot.

We walked through the gate and along a few yards of the grassy lane. Catherine gestured to me to open the metal-barred gate into the horse paddock. I slid the spring-tension bolt, pushed open the heavy squeaking gate and walked through the mud into the field. As two fine chestnut horses and one dappled pony  hurried in curiosity towards us, their owner pointed with the gun barrel towards the stable in the corner of the field nearest to the Deanes' garden. We reached a straw crib where the ground was strewn with a litter of loose straw and had been churned up into messy mud with many hooves.

'Start digging,' she ordered, standing apart but aiming her gun straight at me. She had chosen a good spot. Good for her, not me. No-one would notice the ground being further disturbed there.

I began, although trembling so much I could hardly grip

the spade handle. I toyed with the idea of chucking a spadeful of mud at her, in the manner I had seen in many an action movie. But by the time any would reach her, she would have fired. I dug, and dug. It was hard work. The uncultivated ground was unyielding and large stones clanged against the blade of the spade in nearly every incision. After a time, when the sun was failing and the horses grown bored with watching us, the shallow dip was turning into a hole deep enough require me to stand in it to continue.

Suddenly.

'Mummy!' called a youthful voice. We turned to the source. Melissa and Helena had just entered the paddock and were making towards us with cheery smiles.

'Oh God!' uttered Catherine, utterly deflated.

'Hello! Hi! Great to see you!' I dropped the spade, stepped athletically from the hole, and squelched across the mud towards them as quickly as my legs could move. Then I hugged a rather startled but delighted Melissa as closely as I could. Not – I am ashamed to admit – simply from fondness for the girl, although I loved her more deeply than words could say at that very moment, but as a way of ensuring my own safety.

'Melissa wanted to show me the horses,' explained Helena. 'What are you doing here?'

While I could not speak a word, so choked and tearful with relief, Catherine simply passed us all and made determinedly towards her house, taking no notice of her widely-smiling daughter still locked in my embrace.

After she had left the field, I whispered to a frowning Helena who had caught a glimpse of the firearm in Catherine's clutch. 'Come on, let's take Melissa to our home, right now. No, on no account can she go to hers. Quickly, come on. Now. You don't have a phone on you, do you? Mine's in my bag. I can't get it, not yet. Hurry, come.'

Helena shook her head. Mobile telephones were not objects she had felt any need to acquire.

As we were half way across the Deane family garden lawn, a loud bang, a shot from the direction of the Fletchers' house, stopped us momentarily.

'Come on. Don't think about it. I'll tell you in a minute, but not with Melissa present. Not yet.'

If you have enjoyed the two Julia Deane's books, join the supporters' list now for notification of the publication of the next novel – *Julia's World in Tune*, coming out in 2018.

See www.rosehipbooks.com

Made in the USA
Lexington, KY
23 August 2017